Brown Wolf

And Other Jack London Stories

Jack London

Brown Wolf and Other Jack London Stories

The present edition is a reproduction of previous publication of this classic work. Minor typographical errors may have been corrected without note; however, for an authentic reading experience the spelling, punctuation, and capitalization have been retained from the original text.

ISBN: 978-1-64799-488-4

CONTENTS

INTRODUCTION iv
BROWN WOLF 1
THAT SPOT 14
TRUST 22
ALL GOLD CANYON 33
THE STORY OF KEESH 50
NAM-BOK THE UNVERACIOUS 57
YELLOW HANDKERCHIEF 70
MAKE WESTING 81
THE HEATHEN 88
THE HOBO AND THE FAIRY 105
"JUST MEAT" 117
A NOSE FOR THE KING 132

INTRODUCTION

Boys delight in men who have had adventures, and when they are privileged to read of such exploits in thrilling story form, that is the "seventh heaven" for them. Such a "boys' man" was Jack London, whose whole life was one of stirring action on land and sea. Gifted as a story teller, he wrote books almost without end. Some of them, "The Call of the Wild," "The Sea Wolf" and "White Fang," have already been recognized as fine books for boys. Others, volumes of short stories, contain many of like interest, possessing the same qualities that have made the other and longer stories so acceptable as juveniles.

Effort has been made by the editor to bring together in one volume a number of such stories, not for the reason alone that there might be another Jack London book for boys, but also in order to add to our juvenile literature a volume likely "to be chewed and digested," as Bacon says, a book worthy "to be read whole, and with diligence and attention." For my belief is that boys read altogether too few of such books. Or perhaps it would be more correct to say, have too few opportunities to read such books, because so often we fail to see how quick in their reading their minds are to grasp the more difficult, and how keen and competent their conscience to draw the right conclusion when situations are presented wherein men err so grievously.

It is hoped the stories presented will serve to exercise both the boy's mind and conscience; that seeing and feeling life and nature as Jack London saw and felt it—the best and the worst in human nature, with the Infinite always near and from whom there is no escape—seeing and feeling such things boys will develop the emotional muscles of the spirit, have opened up new windows to their imaginations, and withal add some line or color to their life's ideals.

FRANKLIN K. MATHIEWS, Chief Scout Librarian, Boy Scouts of America.

BROWN WOLF

She had delayed, because of the dew-wet grass, in order to put on her overshoes, and when she emerged from the house found her waiting husband absorbed in the wonder of a bursting almond-bud. She sent a questing glance across the tall grass and in and out among the orchard trees.

"Where's Wolf?" she asked.

"He was here a moment ago." Walt Irvine drew himself away with a jerk from the metaphysics and poetry of the organic miracle of blossom, and surveyed the landscape. "He was running a rabbit the last I saw of him."

"Wolf! Wolf! Here, Wolf!" she called, as they left the clearing and took the trail that led down through the waxen-belled manzanita jungle to the county road.

Irvine thrust between his lips the little finger of each hand and lent to her efforts a shrill whistling.

She covered her ears hastily and made a wry grimace.

"My! for a poet, delicately attuned and all the rest of it, you can make unlovely noises. My eardrums are pierced. You outwhistle——"

"Orpheus."

"I was about to say a street-arab," she concluded severely.

"Poesy does not prevent one from being practical—at least it doesn't prevent me. Mine is no futility of genius that can't sell gems to the magazines."

He assumed a mock extravagance, and went on:

"I am no attic singer, no ballroom warbler. And why? Because I am practical. Mine is no squalor of song that cannot transmute itself, with proper exchange value, into a flower-crowned cottage, a sweet mountain-meadow, a grove of redwoods, an orchard of thirty-seven trees, one long row of blackberries and two short rows of strawberries, to say nothing of a quarter of a mile of gurgling brook."

"Oh, that all your song-transmutations were as successful!" she laughed.

"Name one that wasn't."

"Those two beautiful sonnets that you transmuted into the cow that was accounted the worst milker in the township."

"She was beautiful——" he began.

"But she didn't give milk," Madge interrupted.

"But she was beautiful, now, wasn't she?" he insisted.

"And here's where beauty and utility fall out," was her reply. "And there's the Wolf!"

From the thicket-covered hillside came a crashing of underbrush, and then, forty feet above them, on the edge of the sheer wall of rock, appeared a wolf's head and shoulders. His braced forepaws dislodged a pebble, and with sharp-pricked ears and peering eyes he watched the fall of the pebble till it struck at their feet. Then he transferred his gaze and with open mouth laughed down at them.

"You Wolf, you!" and "You blessed Wolf!" the man and woman called out to him. The ears flattened back and down at the sound, and the head seemed to snuggle under the caress of an invisible hand.

They watched him scramble backward into the thicket, then proceeded on their way. Several minutes later, rounding a turn in the trail where the descent was less precipitous, he joined them in the midst of a miniature avalanche of pebbles and loose soil. He was not demonstrative. A pat and a rub around the ears from the man, and a more prolonged caressing from the woman, and he was away down the trail in front of them, gliding effortlessly over the ground in true wolf fashion.

In build and coat and brush he was a huge timber-wolf; but the lie was given to his wolf-hood by his color and marking. There the dog unmistakably advertised itself. No wolf was ever colored like him. He was brown, deep brown, red-brown, an orgy of browns. Back and shoulders were a warm brown that paled on the sides and underneath to a yellow that was dingy because of the brown that lingered in it. The white of the throat and paws and the spots over the eyes was dirty because of the persistent and ineradicable brown, while the eyes themselves were twin topazes, golden and brown.

The man and woman loved the dog very much; perhaps this was because it had been such a task to win his love. It had been no easy matter when he first drifted in mysteriously out of nowhere to their little mountain cottage. Footsore and famished, he had killed a rabbit under their very noses and under their very windows, and then crawled away and slept by the spring at the foot of the blackberry bushes. When Walt Irvine went down to inspect the intruder, he was snarled at for his pains, and Madge likewise was snarled at when she went down to present, as a peace-offering, a large pan of bread and milk.

A most unsociable dog he proved to be, resenting all their advances, refusing to let them lay hands on him, menacing them with bared fangs and bristling hair. Nevertheless he remained, sleeping and resting by the spring, and eating the food they gave him after they set it down at a safe distance and retreated. His wretched physical condition explained why he lingered; and when he had recuperated, after several days' sojourn, he disappeared.

And this would have been the end of him, so far as Irvine and his wife were concerned, had not Irvine at that particular time been called away into the northern part of the state. Biding along on the train, near to the line between California and Oregon, he chanced to look out of the window and saw his unsociable guest sliding along the wagon road, brown and wolfish, tired yet tireless, dust-covered and soiled with two hundred miles of travel.

Now Irvine was a man of impulse, a poet. He got off the train at the next station, bought a piece of meat at a butcher shop, and captured the vagrant on the outskirts of the town. The return trip was made in the baggage car, and so Wolf came a second time to the mountain cottage. Here he was tied up for a week and made love to by the man and woman. But it was very circumspect love-making. Remote and alien as a traveller from another planet, he snarled down their soft-spoken love-words. He never barked. In all the time they had him he was never known to bark.

To win him became a problem. Irvine liked problems. He had a metal plate made, on which was stamped: "Return to Walt Irvine, Glen Ellen, Sonoma County, California." This was riveted to a collar and strapped about the dog's neck. Then he was turned loose, and promptly He disappeared. A day later came a telegram from Mendocino County. In twenty hours he had made over a hundred miles to the north, and was still going when captured.

He came back by Wells Fargo Express, was tied up three days, and was loosed on the fourth and lost. This time he gained southern Oregon before he was caught and returned. Always, as soon as he received his liberty, he fled away, and always he fled north. He was possessed of an obsession that drove him north. The homing instinct, Irvine called it, after he had expended the selling price of a sonnet in getting the animal back from northern Oregon.

Another time the brown wanderer succeeded in traversing half the length of California, all of Oregon, and most of Washington, before he was picked up and returned "Collect." A remarkable thing was the speed with which he traveled. Fed up and rested, as soon as he was loosed he devoted all his energy to getting over the ground. On the first day's run he was known to cover as high as a hundred and fifty miles, and after that he would average a hundred miles a day until caught. He always arrived back lean and hungry and savage, and always departed fresh and vigorous, cleaving his way northward in response to some prompting of his being that no one could understand.

But at last, after a futile year of flight, he accepted the inevitable and elected to remain at the cottage where first he had killed the rabbit and slept by the spring. Even after that, a long time elapsed before the man and woman succeeded in patting him. It was a great victory, for they alone were allowed to put hands on him. He was fastidiously exclusive, and no guest at the cottage ever succeeded in making up to him. A low growl greeted such approach; if any one had the hardihood to come nearer, the lips lifted, the naked fangs appeared, and the growl became a snarl—a snarl so terrible and malignant that it awed the stoutest of them, as it likewise awed the farmers' dogs that knew ordinary dog snarling, but had never seen wolf snarling before.

He was without antecedents. His history began with Walt and Madge. He had come up from the south, but never a clew did they get of the owner from whom he had evidently fled. Mrs. Johnson, their nearest neighbor and the one who supplied them with milk, proclaimed him a Klondike dog. Her brother was burrowing for frozen pay-streaks in that far country, and so she constituted herself an authority on the subject.

But they did not dispute her. There were the tips of Wolf's ears, obviously so severely frozen at some time that they would never quite heal again. Besides, he looked like the photographs of the Alaskan dogs they saw published in magazines and newspapers. They often speculated over his past, and tried to conjure up (from what they had read and heard) what his northland life had been. That the northland still drew him, they knew; for at night they sometimes heard him crying softly; and when the north wind blew and the bite of frost was in the air, a great restlessness would come upon him and he would lift a mournful lament which they knew to be the long wolf-howl. Yet he never barked. No provocation was great enough to draw from him that canine cry.

Long discussion they had, during the time of winning him, as to whose dog he was. Each claimed him, and each proclaimed loudly any expression of affection made by him. But the man had the better of it at first, chiefly because he was a man. It was patent that Wolf had had no experience with women. He did not understand women. Madge's skirts were something he never quite accepted. The swish of them was enough to set him a-bristle with suspicion, and on a windy day she could not approach him at all.

On the other hand, it was Madge who fed him; also it was she who ruled the kitchen, and it was by her favor, and her favor alone, that he was permitted to come within that sacred precinct. It was because of these things that she bade fair to overcome the handicap of her garments. Then it was that Walt put forth special effort, making it a practice to have Wolf lie at his feet while he wrote, and, between petting and talking, losing much time from his work. Walt won in the end, and his victory was most probably due to the fact that he was a man, though Madge averred that they would have had another quarter of a mile of gurgling brook, and at least two west winds sighing through their redwoods, had Walt properly devoted his energies to song-transmutation and left Wolf alone to exercise a natural taste and an unbiased judgment.

"It's about time I heard from those triolets," Walt said, after a silence of five minutes, during which they had swung steadily down the trail. "There'll be a check at the post office, I know, and we'll transmute it into beautiful buckwheat flour, a gallon of maple syrup, and a new pair of overshoes for you."

"And into beautiful milk from Mrs. Johnson's beautiful cow," Madge added. "To-morrow's the first of the month, you know."

Walt scowled unconsciously; then his face brightened, and he clapped his hand to his breast pocket.

"Never mind. I have here a nice, beautiful, new cow, the best milker in California."

"When did you write it?" she demanded eagerly. Then, reproachfully, "And you never showed it to me."

"I saved it to read to you on the way to the post office, in a spot remarkably like this one," he answered, indicating, with a wave of his hand, a dry log on which to sit.

A tiny stream flowed out of a dense fern-brake, slipped down a mossy-lipped stone, and ran across the path at their feet. From the valley arose the mellow song of meadow larks, while about them, in and out, through sunshine and shadow, fluttered great yellow butterflies.

Up from below came another sound that broke in upon Walt reading softly from his manuscript. It was a crunching of heavy feet, punctuated now and again by the clattering of a displaced stone. As Walt finished and looked to his wife for approval, a man came into view around the turn of the trail. He was bareheaded and sweaty. With a handkerchief in one hand he mopped his face, while in the other hand he carried a new hat and a wilted starched collar which he had removed from his neck. He was a well-built man, and his muscles seemed on the point of bursting out of the painfully new and ready-made black clothes he wore.

"Warm day," Walt greeted him. Walt believed in country democracy, and never missed an opportunity to practice it.

The man paused and nodded.

"I guess I ain't used much to the warm," he vouchsafed half apologetically. "I'm more accustomed to zero weather."

"You don't find any of that in this country," Walt laughed.

"Should say not," the man answered. "An' I ain't here a-lookin' for it neither. I'm tryin' to find my sister. Mebbe you know where she lives. Her name's Johnson, Mrs. William Johnson."

"You're not her Klondike brother!" Madge cried, her eyes bright with interest, "about whom we've heard so much?"

"Yes'm, that's me," he answered modestly. "My name's Miller, Skiff Miller. I just thought I'd s'prise her."

"You are on the right track then. Only you've come by the footpath." Madge stood up to direct him, pointing up the canyon a quarter of a mile. "You see that blasted redwood! Take the little trail turning off to the right. It's the short cut to her house. You can't miss it."

"Yes'm, thank you, ma'am," he said.

He made tentative efforts to go, but seemed awkwardly rooted to the spot. He was gazing at her with an open admiration of which he was quite unconscious, and which was drowning, along with him, in the rising sea of embarrassment in which he floundered.

"We'd like to hear you tell about the Klondike," Madge said. "Mayn't we come over some day while you are at your sister's! Or, better yet, won't you come over and have dinner with us?"

"Yes'm, thank you, ma'am," he mumbled mechanically. Then he caught himself up and added: "I ain't stoppin' long. I got to be pullin' north again. I go out on to-night's train. You see, I've got a mail contract with the government."

When Madge had said that it was too bad, he made another futile effort to go. But he could not take his eyes from her face. He forgot his embarrassment in his admiration, and it was her turn to flush and feel uncomfortable.

It was at this juncture, when Walt had just decided it was time for him to be saying something to relieve the strain, that Wolf, who had been away nosing through the brush, trotted wolf-like into view.

Skiff Miller's abstraction disappeared. The pretty woman before him passed out of his field of vision. He had eyes only for the dog, and a great wonder came into his face.

"Well, I'll be hanged!" he enunciated slowly and solemnly.

He sat down ponderingly on the log, leaving Madge standing. At the sound of his voice, Wolf's ears had flattened down, then his mouth had opened in a laugh. He trotted slowly up to the stranger and first smelled his hands, then licked them with his tongue.

Skiff Miller patted the dog's head, and slowly and solemnly repeated, "Well, I'll be hanged!"

"Excuse me, ma'am," he said the next moment, "I was just s'prised some, that was all."

"We're surprised, too," she answered lightly. "We never saw Wolf make up to a stranger before."

"Is that what you call him—Wolf?" the man asked.

Madge nodded. "But I can't understand his friendliness toward you—unless it's because you're from the Klondike. He's a Klondike dog, you know."

"Yes'm," Miller said absently. He lifted one of Wolf's forelegs and examined the footpads, pressing them and denting them with his thumb. "Kind of soft," he remarked. "He ain't been on trail for a long time."

"I say," Walt broke in, "it is remarkable the way he lets you handle him."

Skiff Miller arose, no longer awkward with admiration of Madge, and in a sharp, businesslike manner asked, "How long have you had him?"

But just then the dog, squirming and rubbing against the newcomer's legs, opened his mouth and barked. It was an explosive bark, brief and joyous, but a bark.

"That's a new one on me," Skiff Miller remarked.

Walt and Madge stared at each other. The miracle had happened. Wolf had barked.

"It's the first time he ever barked," Madge said.

"First time I ever heard him, too," Miller volunteered.

Madge smiled at him. The man was evidently a humorist.

"Of course," she said, "since you have only seen him for five minutes."

Skiff Miller looked at her sharply, seeking in her face the guile her words had led him to suspect.

"I thought you understood," he said slowly. "I thought you'd tumbled to it from his makin' up to me. He's my dog. His name ain't Wolf. It's Brown."

"Oh, Walt!" was Madge's instinctive cry to her husband.

Walt was on the defensive at once.

"How do you know he's your dog?" he demanded.

"Because he is," was the reply.

"Mere assertion," Walt said sharply.

In his slow and pondering way, Skiff Miller looked at him, then asked, with a nod of his head toward Madge:

"How d'you know she's your wife? You just say, 'Because she

is,' and I'll say it's mere assertion. The dog's mine. I bred 'm an' raised 'm, an' I guess I ought to know. Look here. I'll prove it to you."

Skiff Miller turned to the dog. "Brown!" His voice rang out sharply, and at the sound the dog's ears flattened down as to a caress. "Gee!" The dog made a swinging turn to the right. "Now mush-on!" And the dog ceased his swing abruptly and started straight ahead, halting obediently at command.

"I can do it with whistles," Skiff Miller said proudly. "He was my lead dog."

"But you are not going to take him away with you?" Madge asked tremulously.

The man nodded.

"Back into that awful Klondike world of suffering?"

He nodded and added: "Oh, it ain't so bad as all that. Look at me. Pretty healthy specimen, ain't I!"

"But the dogs! The terrible hardship, the heart-breaking toil, the starvation, the frost! Oh, I've read about it and I know."

"I nearly ate him once, over on Little Fish River," Miller volunteered grimly. "If I hadn't got a moose that day was all that saved 'm."

"I'd have died first!" Madge cried.

"Things is different down here," Miller explained. "You don't have to eat dogs. You think different just about the time you're all in. You've never been all in, so you don't know anything about it."

"That's the very point," she argued warmly. "Dogs are not eaten in California. Why not leave him here? He is happy. He'll never want for food—you know that. He'll never suffer from cold and hardship. Here all is softness and gentleness. Neither the human nor nature is savage. He will never know a whip-lash again. And as for the weather—why, it never snows here."

"But it's all-fired hot in summer, beggin' your pardon," Skiff Miller laughed.

"But you do not answer," Madge continued passionately. "What have you to offer him in that northland life?"

"Grub, when I've got it, and that's most of the time," came the answer.

"And the rest of the time?"

"No grub."

"And the work?"

"Yes, plenty of work," Miller blurted out impatiently. "Work without end, an' famine, an' frost, an' all the rest of the miseries—that's what he'll get when he comes with me. But he likes it. He is used to it. He knows that life. He was born to it an' brought up to it. An' you don't know anything about it. You don't know what you're talking about. That's where the dog belongs, and that's where he'll be happiest."

"The dog doesn't go," Walt announced in a determined voice. "So there is no need of further discussion."

"What's that?" Skiff Miller demanded, big brows lowering and an obstinate flush of blood reddening his forehead.

"I said the dog doesn't go, and that settles it. I don't believe he's your dog. You may have seen him sometime. You may even sometime have driven him for his owner. But his obeying the ordinary driving commands of the Alaskan trail is no demonstration that he is yours. Any dog in Alaska would obey you as he obeyed. Besides, he is undoubtedly a valuable dog, as dogs go in Alaska, and that is sufficient explanation of your desire to get possession of him. Anyway, you've got to prove property."

Skiff Miller, cool and collected, the obstinate flush a trifle deeper on his forehead, his huge muscles bulging under the black cloth of his coat, carefully looked the poet up and down as though measuring the strength of his slenderness.

The Klondiker's face took on a contemptuous expression as he said finally: "I reckon there's nothin' in sight to prevent me takin' the dog right here an' now."

Walt's face reddened, and the striking-muscles of his arms and shoulders seemed to stiffen and grow tense. His wife fluttered apprehensively into the breach.

"Maybe Mr. Miller is right," she said. "I am afraid that he is. Wolf does seem to know him, and certainly he answers to the name of 'Brown.' He made friends with him instantly, and you know that's something he never did with anybody before. Besides, look at the way he barked. He was just bursting with joy. Joy over what? Without doubt at finding Mr. Miller."

Walt's striking-muscles relaxed, and his shoulders seemed to droop with hopelessness.

"I guess you're right, Madge," he said. "Wolf isn't Wolf, but Brown, and he must belong to Mr. Miller."

"Perhaps Mr. Miller will sell him," she suggested. "We can buy him."

Skiff Miller shook his head, no longer belligerent, but kindly, quick to be generous in response to generousness.

"I had five dogs," he said, casting about for the easiest way to temper his refusal. "He was the leader. They was the crack team of Alaska. Nothin' could touch 'em. In 1898 I refused five thousand dollars for the bunch. Dogs was high, then, anyway; but that wasn't what made the fancy price. It was the team itself. Brown was the best in the team. That winter I refused twelve hundred for 'm. I didn't sell 'm then, an' I ain't a-sellin' 'm now. Besides, I think a mighty lot of that dog. I've been lookin' for 'm for three years. It made me fair sick when I found he'd been stole—not the value of him, but the—well, I liked 'm so, that's all. I couldn't believe my eyes when I seen 'm just now. I thought I was dreamin'. It was too good to be true. Why, I was his nurse. I put 'm to bed, snug every night. His mother died, and I brought 'm up on condensed milk at two dollars a can when I couldn't afford it in my own coffee. He never knew any mother but me. He used to suck my finger regular, the darn little pup—that finger right there!"

And Skiff Miller, too overwrought for speech, held up a forefinger for them to see.

"That very finger," he managed to articulate, as though it somehow clinched the proof of ownership and the bond of affection.

He was still gazing at his extended finger when Madge began to speak.

"But the dog," she said. "You haven't considered the dog."

Skiff Miller looked puzzled.

"Have you thought about him?" she asked.

"Don't know what you're drivin' at," was the response.

"Maybe the dog has some choice in the matter," Madge went on. "Maybe he has his likes and desires. You have not considered him. You give him no choice. It has never entered your mind that possibly he might prefer California to Alaska. You consider only what you like. You do with him as you would with a sack of potatoes or a bale of hay."

This was a new way of looking at it, and Miller was visibly impressed as he debated it in his mind. Madge took advantage of his indecision.

"If you really love him, what would be happiness to him would be your happiness also," she urged.

Skiff Miller continued to debate with himself, and Madge stole a glance of exultation to her husband, who looked back warm approval.

"What do you think?" the Klondiker suddenly demanded.

It was her turn to be puzzled. "What do you mean?" she asked.

"D'ye think he'd sooner stay in California!"

She nodded her head with positiveness. "I am sure of it."

Skiff Miller again debated with himself, though this time aloud, at the same time running his gaze in a judicial way over the mooted animal.

"He was a good worker. He's done a heap of work for me. He never loafed on me, an' he was a joe-dandy at hammerin' a raw team into shape. He's got a head on him. He can do everything but talk. He knows what you say to him. Look at 'm now. He knows we're talkin' about him."

The dog was lying at Skiff Miller's feet, head close down on paws, ears erect and listening, and eyes that were quick and eager to follow the sound of speech as it fell from the lips of first one and then the other.

"An' there's a lot of work in 'm yet. He's good for years to come. An' I do like him."

Once or twice after that Skiff Miller opened his mouth and closed it again without speaking. Finally he said:

"I'll tell you what I'll do. Your remarks, ma'am, has some weight in them. The dog's worked hard, and maybe he's earned a soft berth an' has got a right to choose. Anyway, we'll leave it up to him. Whatever he says, goes. You people stay right here settin' down. I'll say good-by and walk off casual-like. If he wants to stay, he can stay. If he wants to come with me, let 'm come. I won't call 'm to come an' don't you call 'm to come back."

He looked with sudden suspicion at Madge, and added, "Only you must play fair. No persuadin' after my back is turned."

"We'll play fair," Madge began, but Skiff Miller broke in on her assurances.

"I know the ways of women," he announced. "Their hearts is soft. When their hearts is touched they're likely to stack the cards, look at the bottom of the deck, an' lie—beggin' your pardon, ma'am. I'm only discoursin' about women in general."

"I don't know how to thank you," Madge quavered.

"I don't see as you've got any call to thank me," he replied. "Brown ain't decided yet. Now you won't mind if I go away slow! It's no more'n fair, seein' I'll be out of sight inside a hundred yards."

Madge agreed, and added, "And I promise you faithfully that we won't do anything to influence him."

"Well, then, I might as well he gettin' along," Skiff Miller said in the ordinary tones of one departing.

At this change in his voice, Wolf lifted his head quickly, and still more quickly got to his feet when the man and woman shook hands. He sprang up on his hind legs, resting his fore paws on her hip and at the same time licking Skiff Miller's hand. When the latter shook hands with Walt, Wolf repeated his act, resting his weight on Walt and licking both men's hands.

"It ain't no picnic, I can tell you that," were the Klondiker's last words, as he turned and went slowly up the trail.

For the distance of twenty feet Wolf watched him go, himself all eagerness and expectancy, as though waiting for the man to turn and retrace his steps. Then, with a quick low whine, Wolf sprang after him, overtook him, caught his hand between his teeth with reluctant tenderness, and strove gently to make him pause.

Failing in this, Wolf raced back to where Walt Irvine sat, catching his coat sleeve in his teeth and trying vainly to drag him after the retreating man.

Wolf's perturbation began to wax. He desired ubiquity. He wanted to be in two places at the same time, with the old master and the new, and steadily the distance between them was increasing. He sprang about excitedly, making short nervous leaps and twists, now toward one, now toward the other, in painful indecision, not knowing his own mind, desiring both and unable to choose, uttering quick sharp whines and beginning to pant.

He sat down abruptly on his haunches, thrusting his nose upward, the mouth opening and closing with jerking movements, each time opening wider. These jerking movements were in unison with the recurrent spasms that attacked the throat, each spasm severer and more intense than the preceding one. And in accord with jerks and spasms the larynx began to vibrate, at first silently, accompanied by the rush of air expelled from the lungs, then sounding a low, deep note, the lowest in the register of the human ear. All this was the nervous and muscular preliminary to howling.

But just as the howl was on the verge of bursting from the full throat, the wide-opened mouth was closed, the paroxysms ceased, and he looked long and steadily at the retreating man. Suddenly Wolf turned his head, and over his shoulder just as steadily regarded Walt. The appeal was unanswered. Not a word nor a sign did the dog receive, no suggestion and no clew as to what his conduct should be.

A glance ahead to where the old master was nearing the curve of the trail excited him again. He sprang to his feet with a whine, and then, struck by a new idea, turned his attention to Madge. Hitherto he had ignored her, but now, both masters failing him, she alone was left. He went over to her and snuggled his head in her lap, nudging her arm with his nose—an old trick of his when begging for favors. He backed away from her and began writhing and twisting playfully, curvetting and prancing, half rearing and striking his forepaws to the earth, struggling with all his body, from the wheedling eyes and flattening ears to the wagging tail, to express the thought that was in him and that was denied him utterance.

This, too, he soon abandoned. He was depressed by the

coldness of these humans who had never been cold before. No response could he draw from them, no help could he get. They did not consider him. They were as dead.

He turned and silently gazed after the old master. Skiff Miller was rounding the curve. In a moment he would be gone from view. Yet he never turned his head, plodding straight onward, slowly and methodically, as though possessed of no interest in what was occurring behind his back.

And in this fashion he went out of view. Wolf waited for him to reappear. He waited a long minute, silently, quietly, without movement, as though turned to stone—withal stone quick with eagerness and desire. He barked once, and waited. Then he turned and trotted back to Walt Irvine. He sniffed his hand and dropped down heavily at his feet, watching the trail where it curved emptily from view.

The tiny stream slipping down the mossy-lipped stone seemed suddenly to increase the volume of its gurgling noise. Save for the meadow larks, there was no other sound. The great yellow butterflies drifted silently through the sunshine and lost themselves in the drowsy shadows. Madge gazed triumphantly at her husband.

A few minutes later Wolf got upon his feet. Decision and deliberation marked his movements. He did not glance at the man and woman. His eyes were fixed up the trail. He had made up his mind. They knew it. And they knew, so far as they were concerned, that the ordeal had just begun.

He broke into a trot, and Madge's lips pursed, forming an avenue for the caressing sound that it was the will of her to send forth. But the caressing sound was not made. She was impelled to look at her husband, and she saw the sternness with which he watched her. The pursed lips relaxed, and she sighed inaudibly.

Wolf's trot broke into a run. Wider and wider were the leaps he made. Not once did he turn his head, his wolf's brush standing out straight behind him. He cut sharply across the curve of the trail and was gone.

THAT SPOT

I don't think much of Stephen Mackaye any more, though I used to swear by him. I know that in those days I loved him more than my own brother. If ever I meet Stephen Mackaye again, I shall not be responsible for my actions. It passes beyond me that a man with whom I shared food and blanket, and with whom I mushed over the Chilcoot Trail, should turn out the way he did. I always sized Steve up as a square man, a kindly comrade, without an iota of anything vindictive or malicious in his nature. I shall never trust my judgment in men again. Why, I nursed that man through typhoid fever; we starved together on the headwaters of the Stewart; and he saved my life on the Little Salmon. And now, after the years we were together, all I can say of Stephen Mackaye is that he is the meanest man I ever knew.

We started for the Klondike in the fall rush of 1897, and we started too late to get over Chilcoot Pass before the freeze-up. We packed our outfit on our backs part way over, when the snow began to fly, and then we had to buy dogs in order to sled it the rest of the way. That was how we came to get that Spot. Dogs were high, and we paid one hundred and ten dollars for him. He looked worth it. I say looked, because he was one of the finest appearing dogs I ever saw. He weighed sixty pounds, and he had all the lines of a good sled animal. We never could make out his breed. He wasn't husky, nor Malemute, nor Hudson Bay; he looked like all of them and he didn't look like any of them; and on top of it all he had some of the white man's dog in him, for on one side, in the thick of the mixed yellow-brown-red-and-dirty-white that was his prevailing color, there was a spot of coal-black as big as a water-bucket. That was why we called him Spot.

He was a good looker all right. When he was in condition his muscles stood out in bunches all over him. And he was the strongest looking brute I ever saw in Alaska, also the most intelligent looking. To run your eyes over him, you'd think he could outpull three dogs of his own weight. Maybe he could, but I never saw it. His intelligence didn't run that way. He could steal and forage to perfection; he had an instinct that was positively grewsome for divining when work was to be done and for making a sneak accordingly; and for getting lost and not staying lost he was nothing short of inspired. But when it came to work, the way that intelligence dribbled out of him and left him a mere clot of wobbling, stupid jelly would make your heart bleed.

There are times when I think it wasn't stupidity. Maybe, like some men I know, he was too wise to work. I shouldn't wonder if he put it all over us with that intelligence of his. Maybe he figured it all out and decided that a licking now and again and no work was a whole lot better than work all the time and no licking. He was intelligent enough for such a computation. I tell you, I've sat and looked into that dog's eyes till the shivers ran up and down my spine and the marrow crawled like yeast, what of the intelligence I saw shining out. I can't express myself about that intelligence. It is beyond mere words. I saw it, that's all. At times it was like gazing into a human soul, to look into his eyes; and what I saw there frightened me and started all sorts of ideas in my own mind of reincarnation and all the rest. I tell you I sensed something big in that brute's eyes; there was a message there, but I wasn't big enough myself to catch it. Whatever it was (I know I'm making a fool of myself)—whatever it was, it baffled me. I can't give an inkling of what I saw in that brute's eyes; it wasn't light, it wasn't color; it was something that moved, away back, when the eyes themselves weren't moving. And I guess I didn't see it move, either; I only sensed that it moved. It was an expression,—that's what it was,—and I got an impression of it. No; it was different from a mere expression; it was more than that. I don't know what it was, but it gave me a feeling of kinship just the same. Oh, no, not sentimental kinship. It was, rather, a kinship of equality. Those eyes never pleaded like a deer's eyes. They challenged. No, it wasn't defiance. It was just a calm assumption of equality. And I don't think it was deliberate. My belief is that it was unconscious on his part. It was there because it was there, and it couldn't help shining out. No, I don't mean shine. It didn't shine; it moved. I know I'm talking rot, but if you'd looked into that animal's eyes the way I have, you'd understand. Steve was affected the same way I was. Why, I tried to kill that Spot once—he was no good for anything; and I fell down on it. I led him out into the brush, and he came along slow and unwilling. He knew what was going on. I stopped in a likely place, put my foot on the rope, and pulled my big Colt's. And that dog sat down and looked at me. I tell you he didn't plead. He just looked. And I saw all kinds of incomprehensible things moving, yes, moving, in those eyes of his. I didn't really see them move; I thought I saw them, for, as I said before, I guess I only sensed them. And I want to tell you right now that it got beyond me. It was like killing a man, a conscious, brave man who looked calmly into your gun as much as to say, "Who's afraid?" Then, too, the message seemed so near that, instead of pulling the trigger quick, I stopped to see if I could catch the message. There it was, right before me, glimmering all around in those eyes of his. And then it was too late. I got scared. I was trembly all over, and my stomach generated a nervous palpitation that made me seasick. I just sat down and looked at that dog, and he looked at me, till I thought I was going crazy. Do you want to know what I did? I threw down the gun and ran back to camp with the fear of God in my heart. Steve laughed at me. But I notice that Steve led Spot into the woods, a week later, for the same purpose, and that Steve came back alone, and a little later Spot drifted back, too.

At any rate, Spot wouldn't work. We paid a hundred and ten dollars for him from the bottom of our sack, and he wouldn't work. He wouldn't even tighten the traces. Steve spoke to him the first time we put him in harness, and he sort of shivered, that was all. Not an ounce on the traces. He just stood still and wobbled, like so much jelly. Steve touched him with the whip. He yelped, but not an ounce. Steve touched him again, a bit harder, and he howled—the regular long wolf howl. Then Steve got mad and gave him half a dozen, and I came on the run from the tent. I told Steve he was brutal with the animal, and we had some words—the first we'd ever had. He threw the whip down in the snow, and walked away mad. I picked it up and went to it. That Spot trembled and wobbled and cowered before ever I swung the lash, and with the first bite of it he howled like a lost soul. Next he lay down in the snow. I started the rest of the dogs, and they dragged him along while I threw the whip into him. He rolled over on his back and bumped along, his four legs waving in the air, himself howling as though he was going through a sausage machine. Steve came back and laughed at me, and I apologized for what I'd said.

There was no getting any work out of that Spot; and to make up for it, he was the biggest pig-glutton of a dog I ever saw. On top of that, he was the cleverest thief. There was no circumventing him. Many a breakfast we went without our bacon because Spot had been there first. And it was because of him that we nearly starved to death up the Stewart. He figured out the way to break into our meat-cache, and what he didn't eat, the rest of the team did. But he was impartial. He stole from every body. He was a restless dog always very busy snooping around or going somewhere. And there was never a camp within five miles that he didn't raid. The worst of it was that they always came back on us to pay his board bill, which was just, being the law of the land; but it was mighty hard on us, especially that first winter on the Chilcoot, when we were busted, paying for whole hams and sides of bacon that we never ate. He could fight, too, that Spot. He could do anything but work. He never pulled a pound, but he was the boss of the whole team. The way he made those dogs stand around was an education. He bullied them, and there was always one or more of them fresh-marked with his fangs. But he was more than a bully. He wasn't afraid of anything that walked on four legs; and I've seen him march, single-handed, into a strange team, without any provocation whatever, and put the kibosh on the whole outfit. Did I say he could eat? I caught him eating the whip once. That's straight. He started in at the lash, and when I caught him he was down to the handle, and still going.

But he was a good looker. At the end of the first week we sold him for seventy-five dollars to the Mounted Police. They had experienced dog-drivers, and we knew that by the time he'd covered the six hundred miles to Dawson he'd be a good sled-dog. I say we knew, for we were just getting acquainted with that Spot. A little later we were not brash enough to know anything where he was concerned. A week later we woke up in the morning to the dangdest dog-fight we'd ever heard. It was that Spot came back and knocking the team into shape. We ate a pretty depressing breakfast, I can tell you; but cheered up two hours afterward when we sold him to an official courier, bound in to Dawson with government despatches. That Spot was only three days in coming back, and, as usual, celebrated his arrival with a rough-house.

We spent the winter and spring, after our own outfit was across the pass, freighting other people's outfits; and we made a fat stake. Also, we made money out of Spot. If we sold him once, we sold him twenty times. He always came back, and no one asked for their money. We didn't want the money. We'd have paid handsomely for any one to take him off our hands for keeps. We had to get rid of him, and we couldn't give him away, for that would have been suspicious. But he was such a fine looker that we never had any difficulty in selling him. "Unbroke," we'd say, and they'd pay any old price for him. We sold him as low as twenty-five dollars, and once we got a hundred and fifty for him. That particular party returned him in person, refused to take his money back, and the way he abused us was something awful. He said it was cheap at the price to tell us what he thought of us; and we felt he was so justified that we never talked back. But to this day I've never quite regained all the old self-respect that was mine before that man talked to me.

When the ice cleared out of the lakes and river, we put our outfit in a Lake Bennett boat and started for Dawson. We had a good team of dogs, and of course we piled them on top the outfit. That Spot was along—there was no losing him; and a dozen times, the first day, he knocked one or another of the dogs overboard in the course of fighting with them. It was close quarters, and he didn't like being crowded.

"What that dog needs is space," Steve said the second day. "Let's maroon him."

We did, running the boat in at Caribou Crossing for him to jump ashore. Two of the other dogs, good dogs, followed him; and we lost two whole days trying to find them. We never saw those two dogs again; but the quietness and relief we enjoyed made us decide, like the man who refused his hundred and fifty, that it was cheap at the price. For the first time in months Steve and I laughed and whistled and sang. We were as happy as clams. The dark days were over. The nightmare had been lifted. That Spot was gone.

Three weeks later, one morning, Steve and I were standing on the river-bank at Dawson. A small boat was just arriving from Lake Bennett. I saw Steve give a start, and heard him say something that was not nice and that was not under his breath. Then I looked; and there, in the bow of the boat, with ears pricked up, sat Spot. Steve and I sneaked immediately, like beaten curs, like cowards, like absconders from justice. It was this last that the lieutenant of police thought when he saw us sneaking. He surmised that there was law-officers in the boat who were after us. He didn't wait to find out, but kept us in sight, and in the M. & M. saloon got us in a corner. We had a merry time explaining, for we refused to go back to the boat and meet Spot; and finally he held us under guard of another policeman while he went to the boat. After we got clear of him, we started for the cabin, and when we arrived, there was that Spot sitting on the stoop waiting for us. Now how did he know we lived there? There were forty thousand people in Dawson that summer, and how did he savve our cabin out of all the cabins? How did he know we were in Dawson, anyway? I leave it to you. But don't forget what I have said about his intelligence and that immortal something I have seen glimmering in his eyes.

There was no getting rid of him any more. There were too many people in Dawson who had bought him up on Chilcoot, and the story got around. Half a dozen times we put him on board steamboats going down the Yukon; but he merely went ashore at the first landing and trotted back up the bank. We couldn't sell him, we couldn't kill him (both Steve and I had tried), and nobody else was able to kill him. He bore a charmed life. I've seen him go down in a dog-fight on the main street with fifty dogs on top of him, and when they were separated, he'd appear on all his four legs, unharmed, while two of the dogs that had been on top of him would be lying dead.

I saw him steal a chunk of moose meat from Major Dinwiddie's cache so heavy that he could just keep one jump ahead of Mrs. Dinwiddie's squaw cook, who was after him with an axe. As he went up the hill, after the squaw gave up, Major Dinwiddie himself came out and pumped his Winchester into the landscape. He emptied his magazine twice, and never touched that Spot. Then a policeman came along and arrested him for discharging firearms inside the city limits. Major Dinwiddie paid his fine, and Steve and I paid him for the moose meat at the rate of a dollar a pound, bones and all. That was what he paid for it. Meat was high that year.

I am only telling what I saw with my own eyes. And now I'll tell you something also. I saw that Spot fall through a water-hole. The ice was three and a half feet thick, and the current sucked him under like a straw. Three hundred yards below was the big water-hole used by the hospital. Spot crawled out of the hospital water-hole, licked off the water, bit out the ice that had formed between his toes, trotted up the bank, and whipped a big Newfoundland belonging to the Gold Commissioner.

In the fall of 1898, Steve and I poled up the Yukon on the last water, bound for Stewart River. We took the dogs along, all except Spot. We figured we'd been feeding him long enough. He'd cost us more time and trouble and money and grub than we'd got by selling him on the Chilcoot—especially grub. So Steve and I tied him down in the cabin and pulled our freight. We camped that night at the mouth of Indian River, and Steve and I were pretty facetious over having shaken him. Steve was a funny fellow, and I was just sitting up in the blankets and laughing when a tornado hit camp. The way that Spot walked into those dogs and gave them what-for was hair-raising. Now how did he get loose? It's up to you. I haven't any theory. And how did he get across the Klondike River? That's another facer. And anyway, how did he know we had gone up the Yukon? You see, we went by water, and he couldn't smell our tracks. Steve and I began to get superstitious about that dog. He got on our nerves, too; and, between you and me, we were just a mite afraid of him.

The freeze-up came on when we were at the mouth of Henderson Creek, and we traded him off for two sacks of flour to an outfit that was bound up White River after copper. Now that whole outfit was lost. Never trace nor hide nor hair of men, dogs, sleds, or anything was ever found. They dropped clean out of sight. It became one of the mysteries of the country. Steve and I plugged away up the Stewart, and six weeks afterward that Spot crawled into camp. He was a perambulating skeleton, and could just drag along; but he got there. And what I want to know is who told him we were up the Stewart? We could have gone a thousand other places. How did he know? You tell me, and I'll tell you.

No losing him. At the Mayo he started a row with an Indian dog. The buck who owned the dog took a swing at Spot with an axe, missed him, and killed his own dog. Talk about magic and turning bullets aside—I, for one, consider it a blamed sight harder to turn an axe aside with a big buck at the other end of it. And I saw him do it with my own eyes. That buck didn't want to kill his own dog. You've got to show me.

I told you about Spot breaking into our meat-cache. It was nearly the death of us. There wasn't any more meat to be killed and meat was all we had to live on. The moose had gone back several hundred miles and the Indians with them. There we were. Spring was on and we had to wait for the river to break. We got pretty thin before we decided to eat the dogs, and we decided to eat Spot first. Do you know what that dog did? He sneaked. Now how did he know our minds were made up to eat him? We sat up nights laying for him, but he never came back, and we ate the other dogs. We ate the whole team.

And now for the sequel. You know what it is when a big river breaks up and a few billion tons of ice go out, jamming and milling and grinding. Just in the thick of it, when the Stewart went out, rumbling and roaring, we sighted Spot out in the middle. He'd got caught as he was trying to cross up above somewhere. Steve and I yelled and shouted and ran up and down the bank, tossing our hats in the air. Sometimes we'd stop and hug each other, we were that boisterous, for we saw Spot's finish. He didn't have a chance in a million. He didn't have any chance at all. After the ice-run, we got into a canoe and paddled down to the Yukon, and down the Yukon to Dawson, stopping to feed up for a week at the cabins at the mouth of Henderson Creek. And as we came in to the bank at Dawson, there sat that Spot, waiting for us, his ears pricked up, his tail wagging, his mouth smiling, extending a hearty welcome to us. Now how did he get out of that ice? How did he know we were coming to Dawson, to the very hour and minute, to be out there on the bank waiting for us?

The more I think of that Spot, the more I am convinced that there are things in this world that go beyond science. On no scientific grounds can that Spot be explained. It's psychic phenomena, or mysticism, or something of that sort, I guess, with a lot of Theosophy thrown in. The Klondike is a good country. I might have been there yet, and become a millionaire, if it hadn't been for

Spot. He got on my nerves. I stood him for two years all together, and then I guess my stamina broke. It was the summer of 1899 when I pulled out. I didn't say anything to Steve. I just sneaked. But I fixed it up all right. I wrote Steve a note, and enclosed a package of "rough-on-rats," telling him what to do with it. I was worn down to skin and bone by that Spot, and I was that nervous that I'd jump and look around when there wasn't anybody within hailing distance. But it was astonishing the way I recuperated when I got quit of him. I got back twenty pounds before I arrived in San Francisco, and by the time I'd crossed the ferry to Oakland I was my old self again, so that even my wife looked in vain for any change in me.

Steve wrote to me once, and his letter seemed irritated. He took it kind of hard because I'd left him with Spot. Also, he said he'd used the "rough-on-rats," per directions, and that there was nothing doing. A year went by. I was back in the office and prospering in all ways—even getting a bit fat. And then Steve arrived. He didn't look me up. I read his name in the steamer list, and wondered why. But I didn't wonder long. I got up one morning and found that Spot chained to the gatepost and holding up the milkman. Steve went north to Seattle, I learned, that very morning. I didn't put on any more weight. My wife made me buy him a collar and tag, and within an hour he showed his gratitude by killing her pet Persian cat. There is no getting rid of that Spot. He will be with me until I die, for he'll never die. My appetite is not so good since he arrived, and my wife says I am looking peaked. Last night that Spot got into Mr. Harvey's hen-house (Harvey is my next door neighbor) and killed nineteen of his fancy-bred chickens. I shall have to pay for them. My neighbors on the other side quarreled with my wife and then moved out. Spot was the cause of it. And that is why I am disappointed in Stephen Mackaye. I had no idea he was so mean a man.

TRUST

All lines had been cast off, and the Seattle No. 4 was pulling slowly out from the shore. Her decks were piled high with freight and baggage, and swarmed with a heterogeneous company of Indians, dogs, and dog-mushers, prospectors, traders, and homeward-bound gold-seekers. A goodly portion of Dawson was lined up on the bank, saying good-by. As the gang-plank came in and the steamer nosed into the stream, the clamor of farewell became deafening. Also, in that eleventh moment, everybody began to remember final farewell messages and to shout them back and forth across the widening stretch of water. Louis Bondell, curling his yellow mustache with one hand and languidly waving the other hand to his friends on shore, suddenly remembered something and sprang to the rail.

"Oh, Fred!" he bawled. "Oh, Fred!"

The "Fred" desired thrust a strapping pair of shoulders through the forefront of the crowd on the bank and tried to catch Louis Bondell's message. The latter grew red in the face with vain vociferation. Still the water widened between steamboat and shore.

"Hey you, Captain Scott!" he yelled at the pilot-house. "Stop the boat!"

The gongs clanged, and the big stern wheel reversed, then stopped. All hands on steamboat and on bank took advantage of this respite to exchange final, new, and imperative farewells. More futile than ever was Louis Bondell's effort to make himself heard. The Seattle No. 4 lost way and drifted down-stream, and Captain Scott had to go ahead and reverse a second time. His head disappeared inside the pilot-house, coming into view a moment later behind a big megaphone.

Now Captain Scott had a remarkable voice, and the "Shut up!" he launched at the crowd on deck and on shore could have been heard at the top of Moosehide Mountain and as far as Klondike City. This official remonstrance from the pilot-house spread a film of silence over the tumult.

"Now, what do you want to say?" Captain Scott demanded.

"Tell Fred Churchill—he's on the bank there—tell him to go to Macdonald. It's in his safe—a small gripsack of mine. Tell him to get it and bring it out when he comes."

In the silence Captain Scott bellowed the message ashore through the megaphone:—

"You, Fred Churchill, go to Macdonald—in his safe—small

gripsack—belongs to Louis Bondell—important! Bring it out when you come! Got it?"

Churchill waved his hand in token that he had got it. In truth, had Macdonald, half a mile away, opened his window, he'd have got it, too. The tumult of farewell rose again, the gongs clanged, and the Seattle No. 4 went ahead, swung out into the stream, turned on her heel, and headed down the Yukon, Bondell and Churchill waving farewell and mutual affection to the last.

That was in midsummer. In the fall of the year, the W.H. Willis started up the Yukon with two hundred homeward-bound pilgrims on board. Among them was Churchill. In his stateroom, in the middle of a clothes-bag, was Louis Bondell's grip. It was a small, stout leather affair, and its weight of forty pounds always made Churchill nervous when he wandered too far from it. The man in the adjoining stateroom had a treasure of gold-dust hidden similarly in a clothes-bag, and the pair of them ultimately arranged to stand watch and watch. While one went down to eat, the other kept an eye on the two stateroom doors. When Churchill wanted to take a hand at whist, the other man mounted guard, and when the other man wanted to relax his soul, Churchill read four-months'-old newspapers on a camp stool between the two doors.

There were signs of an early winter, and the question that was discussed from dawn till dark, and far into the dark, was whether they would get out before the freeze-up or be compelled to abandon the steamboat and tramp out over the ice. There were irritating delays. Twice the engines broke down and had to be tinkered up, and each time there were snow flurries to warn them of the imminence of winter. Nine times the W.H. Willis essayed to ascend the Five-Finger Rapids with her impaired machinery, and when she succeeded, she was four days behind her very liberal schedule. The question that then arose was whether or not the steamboat Flora would wait for her above the Box Cañon. The stretch of water between the head of the Box Cañon and the foot of the White Horse Rapids was unnavigable for steamboats and passengers were transshipped at that point, walking around the rapids from one steamboat to the other. There were no telephones in the country, hence no way of informing the waiting Flora that the Willis was four days late, but coming.

When the W.H. Willis pulled into White Horse, it was learned that the Flora had waited three days over the limit, and had departed only a few hours before. Also, it was learned that she would tie up at Tagish Post till nine o'clock, Sunday morning. It was then four o'clock Saturday afternoon. The pilgrims called a meeting.

On board was a large Peterborough canoe, consigned to the police post at the head of Lake Bennett. They agreed to be responsible for it and to deliver it. Next, they called for volunteers. Two men were needed to make a race for the Flora. A score of men volunteered on the instant. Among them was Churchill, such being his nature that he volunteered before he thought of Bondell's gripsack. When this thought came to him, he began to hope that he would not be selected; but a man who had made a name as captain of a college football eleven, as a president of an athletic club, as a dog-musher and a stampeder in the Yukon, and, moreover, who possessed such shoulders as he, had no right to avoid the honor. It was thrust upon him and upon a gigantic German, Nick Antonsen.

While a crowd of the pilgrims, the canoe on their shoulders, started on a trot over the portage, Churchill ran to his stateroom. He turned the contents of the clothes-bag on the floor and caught up the grip with the intention of intrusting it to the man next door. Then the thought smote him that it was not his grip, and that he had no right to let it out of his own possession. So he dashed ashore with it and ran up the portage, changing it often from one hand to the other, and wondering if it really did not weigh more than forty pounds.

It was half-past four in the afternoon when the two men started. The current of the Thirty Mile River was so strong that rarely could they use the paddles. It was out on one bank with a tow-line over the shoulders stumbling over the rocks, forcing a way through the underbrush, slipping at times and falling into the water, wading often up to the knees and waist; and then, when an insurmountable bluff was encountered, it was into the canoe, out paddles, and a wild and losing dash across the current to the other bank, in paddles, over the side, and out tow-line again. It was exhausting work. Antonsen toiled like the giant he was, uncomplaining, persistent, but driven to his utmost by the powerful body and indomitable brain of Churchill. They never paused for rest. It was go, go, and keep on going. A crisp wind blew down the river, freezing their hands and making it imperative, from time to time, to beat the blood back into the numb fingers. As night came on, they were compelled to trust to luck. They fell repeatedly on the untraveled banks and tore their clothing to shreds in the underbrush they could not see. Both men were badly scratched and bleeding. A dozen times, in their wild dashes from bank to bank, they struck snags and were capsized. The first time this happened, Churchill dived and groped in three feet of water for the gripsack. He lost half an hour in recovering it, and after that it was carried securely lashed to the canoe. As long as the canoe floated it was safe. Antonsen jeered at the grip, and toward morning began to abuse it; but Churchill vouchsafed no explanations.

Their delays and mischances were endless. On one swift bend, around which poured a healthy young rapid, they lost two hours, making a score of attempts and capsizing twice. At this point, on both banks, were precipitous bluffs, rising out of deep water, and along which they could neither tow nor pole, while they could not gain with the paddles against the current. At each attempt they strained to the utmost with the paddles, and each time, with hearts nigh to bursting from the effort, they were played out and swept back. They succeeded finally by an accident. In the swiftest current, near the end of another failure, a freak of the current sheered the canoe out of Churchill's control and flung it against the bluff. Churchill made a blind leap at the bluff and landed in a crevice. Holding on with one hand, he held the swamped canoe with the other till Antonsen dragged himself out of the water. Then they pulled the canoe out and rested. A fresh start at this crucial point took them by. They landed on the bank above and plunged immediately ashore and into the brush with the tow-line.

Daylight found them far below Tagish Post. At nine o 'clock Sunday morning they could hear the Flora whistling her departure. And when, at ten o'clock, they dragged themselves in to the Post, they could just barely see the Flora's smoke far to the southward. It was a pair of worn-out tatterdemalions that Captain Jones of the Mounted Police welcomed and fed, and he afterward averred that they possessed two of the most tremendous appetites he had ever observed. They lay down and slept in their wet rags by the stove. At the end of two hours Churchill got up, carried Bondell's grip, which he had used for a pillow, down to the canoe, kicked Antonsen awake, and started in pursuit of the Flora.

"There's no telling what might happen—machinery break down or something," was his reply to Captain Jones's expostulations. "I'm going to catch that steamer and send her back for the boys."

Tagish Lake was white with a fall gale that blew in their teeth. Big, swinging seas rushed upon the canoe, compelling one man to bail and leaving one man to paddle. Headway could not be made. They ran along the shallow shore and went overboard, one man ahead on the tow-line, the other shoving on the canoe. They fought the gale up to their waists in the icy water, often up to their necks, often over their heads and buried by the big, crested waves. There was no rest, never a moment's pause from the cheerless, heart-breaking battle. That night, at the head of Tagish Lake, in the thick of a driving snow-squall, they overhauled the Flora. Antonsen fell on board, lay where he had fallen, and snored. Churchill looked like a wild man. His clothes barely clung to him. His face was iced up and swollen from the protracted effort of twenty-four hours, while his hands were so swollen that he could not close the fingers. As for his feet, it was an agony to stand upon them.

The captain of the Flora was loath to go back to White Horse. Churchill was persistent and imperative; the captain was stubborn. He pointed out finally that nothing was to be gained by going back, because the only ocean steamer at Dyea, the Athenian, was to sail on Tuesday morning, and that he could not make the back trip to White Horse and bring up the stranded pilgrims in time to make the connection.

"What time does the Athenian sail?" Churchill demanded.

"Seven o'clock, Tuesday morning."

"All right," Churchill said, at the same time kicking a tattoo on the ribs of the snoring Antonsen. "You go back to White Horse. We'll go ahead and hold the Athenian."

Antonsen, stupid with sleep, not yet clothed in his waking mind, was bundled into the canoe, and did not realize what had happened till he was drenched with the icy spray of a big sea, and heard Churchill snarling at him through the darkness:—

"Paddle, can't you! Do you want to be swamped?"

Daylight found them at Caribou Crossing, the wind dying down, and Antonsen too far gone to dip a paddle. Churchill grounded the canoe on a quiet beach, where they slept. He took the precaution of twisting his arm under the weight of his head. Every few minutes the pain of the pent circulation aroused him, whereupon he would look at his watch and twist the other arm under his head. At the end of two hours he fought with Antonsen to rouse him. Then they started. Lake Bennett, thirty miles in length, was like a mill-pond; but, halfway across, a gale from the south smote them and turned the water white. Hour after hour they repeated the struggle on Tagish, over the side, pulling and shoving on the canoe, up to their waists and necks, and over their heads, in the icy water; toward the last the good-natured giant played completely out. Churchill drove him mercilessly; but when he pitched forward and bade fair to drown in three feet of water, the other dragged him into the canoe. After that, Churchill fought on alone, arriving at the police post at the head of Bennett in the early afternoon. He tried to help Antonsen out of the canoe, but failed. He listened to the exhausted man's heavy breathing, and envied him when he thought of what he himself had yet to undergo. Antonsen could lie there and sleep; but he, behind time, must go on over mighty Chilcoot and down to the sea. The real struggle lay before him, and he almost regretted the strength that resided in his frame because of the torment it could inflict upon that frame.

Churchill pulled the canoe up on the beach, seized Bondell's grip, and started on a limping dog-trot for the police post.

"There's a canoe down there, consigned to you from Dawson," he hurled at the officer who answered his knock. "And there's a man in it pretty near dead. Nothing serious; only played out. Take care of him. I've got to rush. Good-by. Want to catch the Athenian."

A mile portage connected Lake Bennett and Lake Linderman, and his last words he flung back after him as he resumed the trot. It was a very painful trot, but he clenched his teeth and kept on, forgetting his pain most of the time in the fervent heat with which he regarded the gripsack. It was a severe handicap. He swung it from one hand to the other, and back again. He tucked it under his arm. He threw one hand over the opposite shoulder, and the bag bumped and pounded on his back as he ran along. He could scarcely hold it in his bruised and swollen fingers, and several times he dropped it. Once, in changing from one hand to the other, it escaped his clutch and fell in front of him, tripped him up, and threw him violently to the ground.

At the far end of the portage he bought an old set of pack-straps for a dollar, and in them he swung the grip. Also, he chartered a launch to run him the six miles to the upper end of Lake Linderman, where he arrived at four in the afternoon. The Athenian was to sail from Dyea next morning at seven. Dyea was twenty-eight miles away, and between towered Chilcoot. He sat down to adjust his foot-gear for the long climb, and woke up. He had dozed the instant he sat down, though he had not slept thirty seconds. He was afraid his next doze might be longer, so he finished fixing his foot-gear standing up. Even then he was overpowered for a fleeting moment. He experienced the flash of unconsciousness; becoming aware of it, in midair, as his relaxed body was sinking to the ground and as he caught himself together, he stiffened his muscles with a spasmodic wrench, and escaped the fall. The sudden jerk back to consciousness left him sick and trembling. He beat his head with the heel of his hand, knocking wakefulness into the numb brain.

Jack Burns's pack-train was starting back light for Crater Lake, and Churchill was invited to a mule. Burns wanted to put the gripsack on another animal, but Churchill held on to it, carrying it on his saddle-pommel. But he dozed, and the grip persisted in dropping off the pommel, one side or the other, each time wakening him with a sickening start. Then, in the early darkness, Churchill's mule brushed him against a projecting branch that laid his cheek open. To cap it, the mule blundered off the trail and fell, throwing rider and gripsack out upon the rocks. After that, Churchill walked, or stumbled, rather, over the apology for a trail, leading the mule. Stray and awful odors, drifting from each side the trail, told of the horses that had died in the rush for gold. But he did not mind. He was too sleepy. By the time Long Lake was reached, however, he had recovered from his sleepiness; and at Deep Lake he resigned the gripsack to Burns. But thereafter, by the light of the dim stars, he kept his eyes on Burns. There were not going to be any accidents with that bag.

At Crater Lake the pack-train went into camp, and Churchill, slinging the grip on his back, started the steep climb for the summit. For the first time, on that precipitous wall, he realized how tired he was. He crept and crawled like a crab, burdened by the weight of his limbs. A distinct and painful effort of will was required each time he lifted a foot. An hallucination came to him that he was shod with lead, like a deep-sea diver, and it was all he could do to resist the desire to reach down and feel the lead. As for Bondell's gripsack, it was inconceivable that forty pounds could weigh so much. It pressed him down like a mountain, and he looked back with unbelief to the year before, when he had climbed that same pass with a hundred and fifty pounds on his back, If those loads had weighed a hundred and fifty pounds, then Bondell's grip weighed five hundred.

The first rise of the divide from Crater Lake was across a small glacier. Here was a well-defined trail. But above the glacier, which was also above timber-line, was naught but a chaos of naked rock and enormous boulders. There was no way of seeing the trail in the darkness, and he blundered on, paying thrice the ordinary exertion for all that he accomplished. He won the summit in the thick of howling wind and driving snow, providentially stumbling upon a small, deserted tent, into which he crawled. There he found and bolted some ancient fried potatoes and half a dozen raw eggs.

When the snow ceased and the wind eased down, he began the almost impossible descent. There was no trail, and he stumbled and blundered, often finding himself, at the last moment, on the edge of rocky walls and steep slopes the depth of which he had no way of judging. Part way down, the stars clouded over again, and in the consequent obscurity he slipped and rolled and slid for a hundred feet, landing bruised and bleeding on the bottom of a large shallow hole. From all about him arose the stench of dead horses. The hole was handy to the trail, and the packers had made a practice of tumbling into it their broken and dying animals. The stench overpowered him, making him deathly sick, and as in a nightmare he scrambled out. Halfway up, he recollected Bondell's gripsack. It had fallen into the hole with him; the pack-strap had evidently broken, and he had forgotten it. Back he went into the pestilential charnel-pit, where he crawled around on hands and knees and groped for half an hour. Altogether he encountered and counted seventeen dead horses (and one horse still alive that he shot with his revolver) before he found Bondell's grip. Looking back upon a life that had not been without valor and achievement, he unhesitatingly declared to himself that this return after the grip was the most heroic act he had ever performed. So heroic was it that he was twice on the verge of fainting before he crawled out of the hole.

By the time he had descended to the Scales, the steep pitch of Chilcoot was past, and the way became easier. Not that it was an easy way, however, in the best of places; but it became a really possible trail, along which he could have made good time if he had not been worn out, if he had had light with which to pick his steps, and if it had not been for Bondell's gripsack. To him, in his exhausted condition, it was the last straw. Having barely strength to carry himself along, the additional weight of the grip was sufficient to throw him nearly every time he tripped or stumbled. And when he escaped tripping, branches reached out in the darkness, hooked the grip between his shoulders, and held him back.

His mind was made up that if he missed the Athenian it would be the fault of the gripsack. In fact, only two things remained in his consciousness—Bondell's grip and the steamer. He knew only those two things, and they became identified, in a way, with some stern mission upon which he had journeyed and toiled for centuries. He walked and struggled on as in a dream. A part of the dream was his arrival at Sheep Camp. He stumbled into a saloon, slid his shoulders out of the straps, and started to deposit the grip at his feet. But it slipped from his fingers and struck the floor with a heavy thud that was not unnoticed by two men who were just leaving. Churchill drank a glass of whiskey, told the barkeeper to call him in ten minutes, and sat down, his feet on the grip, his head on his knees.

So badly did his misused body stiffen, that when he was called it required another ten minutes and a second glass of whiskey to unbend his joints and limber up the muscles.

"Hey! not that way!" the barkeeper shouted, and then went after him and started him through the darkness toward Canyon

City. Some little husk of inner consciousness told Churchill that the direction was right, and, still as in a dream, he took the canyon trail. He did not know what warned him, but after what seemed several centuries of travelling, he sensed danger and drew his revolver. Still in the dream, he saw two men step out and heard them halt him. His revolver went off four times, and he saw the flashes and heard the explosions of their revolvers. Also, he was aware that he had been hit in the thigh. He saw one man go down, and, as the other came for him, he smashed him a straight blow with the heavy revolver full in the face. Then he turned and ran. He came from the dream shortly afterward, to find himself plunging down the trail at a limping lope. His first thought was for the gripsack. It was still on his back. He was convinced that what had happened was a dream till he felt for his revolver and found it gone. Next he became aware of a sharp stinging of his thigh, and after investigating, he found his hand warm with blood. It was a superficial wound, but it was incontestable. He became wider awake, and kept up the lumbering run to Canyon City.

He found a man, with a team of horses and a wagon, who got out of bed and harnessed up for twenty dollars. Churchill crawled in on the wagon-bed and slept, the gripsack still on his back. It was a rough ride, over water-washed boulders down the Dyea Valley; but he roused only when the wagon hit the highest places. Any altitude of his body above the wagon-bed of less than a foot did not faze him. The last mile was smooth going, and he slept soundly.

He came to in the gray dawn, the driver shaking him savagely and howling into his ear that the Athenian was gone. Churchill looked blankly at the deserted harbor.

"There's a smoke over at Skaguay," the man said.

Churchill's eyes were too swollen to see that far, but he said: "It's she. Get me a boat."

The driver was obliging, and found a skiff and a man to row it for ten dollars, payment in advance. Churchill paid, and was helped into the skiff. It was beyond him to get in by himself. It was six miles to Skaguay, and he had a blissful thought of sleeping those six miles. But the man did not know how to row, and Churchill took the oars and toiled for a few more centuries. He never knew six longer and more excruciating miles. A snappy little breeze blew up the inlet and held him back. He had a gone feeling at the pit of the stomach, and suffered from faintness and numbness. At his command, the man took the bailer and threw salt water into his face.

The Athenian's anchor was up-and-down when they came alongside, and Churchill was at the end of his last remnant of strength.

"Stop her! Stop her!" he shouted hoarsely. "Important message! Stop her!"

Then he dropped his chin on his chest and slept. "When half a dozen men started to carry him up the gang-plank, he awoke, reached for the grip, and clung to it like a drowning man. On deck he became a center of horror and curiosity. The clothing in which he had left White Horse was represented by a few rags, and he was as frayed as his clothing. He had traveled for fifty-five hours at the top notch of endurance. He had slept six hours in that time, and he was twenty pounds lighter than when he started. Face and hands and body were scratched and bruised, and he could scarcely see. He tried to stand up, but failed, sprawling out on the deck, hanging on to the gripsack, and delivering his message.

"Now, put me to bed," he finished; "I'll eat when I wake up."

They did him honor, carrying him down in his rags and dirt and depositing him and Bondell's grip in the bridal chamber, which was the biggest and most luxurious stateroom in the ship. Twice he slept the clock around, and he had bathed and shaved and eaten and was leaning over the rail smoking a cigar when the two hundred pilgrims from White Horse came alongside.

By the time the Athenian arrived in Seattle, Churchill had fully recuperated, and he went ashore with Bondell's grip in his hand. He felt proud of that grip. To him it stood for achievement and integrity and trust. "I've delivered the goods," was the way he expressed these various high terms to himself. It was early in the evening, and he went straight to Bondell's home. Louis Bondell was glad to see him, shaking hands with both hands at the same time and dragging him into the house.

"Oh, thanks, old man; it was good of you to bring it out," Bondell said when he received the gripsack.

He tossed it carelessly upon a couch, and Churchill noted with an appreciative eye the rebound of its weight from the springs. Bondell was volleying him with questions.

"How did you make out? How're the boys! What became of Bill Smithers? Is Del Bishop still with Pierce? Did he sell my dogs? How did Sulphur Bottom show up? You're looking fine. What steamer did you come out on?"

To all of which Churchill gave answer, till half an hour had gone by and the first lull in the conversation had arrived.

"Hadn't you better take a look at it?" he suggested, nodding his head at the gripsack.

"Oh, it's all right," Bondell answered. "Did Mitchell's dump turn out as much as he expected?"

"I think you'd better look at it," Churchill insisted. "When I deliver a thing, I want to be satisfied that it's all right. There's always the chance that somebody might have got into it when I was asleep, or something."

"It's nothing important, old man," Bondell answered, with a laugh.

"Nothing important," Churchill echoed in a faint, small voice. Then he spoke with decision: "Louis, what's in that bag? I want to know."

Louis looked at him curiously, then left the room and returned with a bunch of keys. He inserted his hand and drew out a heavy .44 Colt's revolver. Next came out a few boxes of ammunition for the revolver and several boxes of Winchester cartridges.

Churchill took the gripsack and looked into it. Then he turned it upside down and shook it gently.

"The gun's all rusted," Bondell said. "Must have been out in the rain."

"Yes," Churchill answered. "Too bad it got wet. I guess I was a bit careless."

He got up and went outside. Ten minutes later Louis Bondell went out and found him on the steps, sitting down, elbows on knees and chin on hands, gazing steadfastly out into the darkness.

ALL GOLD CANYON

It was the green heart of the canyon, where the walls swerved back from the rigid plan and relieved their harshness of line by making a little sheltered nook and filling it to the brim with sweetness and roundness and softness. Here all things rested. Even the narrow stream ceased its turbulent down-rush long enough to form a quiet pool. Knee-deep in the water, with drooping head and half-shut eyes, drowsed a red-coated, many-antlered buck.

On one side, beginning at the very lip of the pool, was a tiny meadow, a cool, resilient surface of green that extended to the base of the frowning wall. Beyond the pool a gentle slope of earth ran up and up to meet the opposing wall. Fine grass covered the slope—grass that was spangled with flowers, with here and there patches of color, orange and purple and golden. Below, the canyon was shut in. There was no view. The walls leaned together abruptly and the canyon ended in a chaos of rocks, moss-covered and hidden by a green screen of vines and creepers and boughs of trees. Up the canyon rose far hills and peaks, the big foothills, pine-covered and remote. And far beyond, like clouds upon the border of the sky, towered minarets of white, where the Sierra's eternal snows flashed austerely the blazes of the sun.

There was no dust in the canyon. The leaves and flowers were clean and virginal. The grass was young velvet. Over the pool three cottonwoods sent their snowy fluffs fluttering down the quiet air. On the slope the blossoms of the wine-wooded manzanita filled the air with springtime odors, while the leaves, wise with experience, were already beginning their vertical twist against the coming aridity of summer. In the open spaces on the slope, beyond the farthest shadow-reach of the manzanita, poised the mariposa lilies, like so many flights of jewelled moths suddenly arrested and on the verge of trembling into flight again. Here and there that woods harlequin, the madrone, permitting itself to be caught in the act of changing its pea-green trunk to madder-red, breathed its fragrance into the air from great clusters of waxen bells. Creamy white were these bells, shaped like lilies-of-the-valley, with the sweetness of perfume that is of the springtime.

There was not a sigh of wind. The air was drowsy with its weight of perfume. It was a sweetness that would have been cloying had the air been heavy and humid. But the air was sharp and thin. It was as starlight transmuted into atmosphere, shot through and warmed by sunshine, and flower-drenched with sweetness.

An occasional butterfly drifted in and out through the patches of light and shade. And from all about rose the low and sleepy hum of mountain bees—feasting Sybarites that jostled one another good-naturedly at the board, nor found time for rough discourtesy. So quietly did the little stream drip and ripple its way through the canyon that it spoke only in faint and occasional gurgles. The voice of the stream was as a drowsy whisper, ever interrupted by dozings and silences, ever lifted again in the awakenings.

The motion of all things was a drifting in the heart of the canyon. Sunshine and butterflies drifted in and out among the trees. The hum of the bees and the whisper of the stream were a drifting of sound. And the drifting sound and drifting color seemed to weave together in the making of a delicate and intangible fabric which was the spirit of the place. It was a spirit of peace that was not of death, but of smooth-pulsing life, of quietude that was not silence, of movement that was not action, of repose that was quick with existence without being violent with struggle and travail. The spirit of the place was the spirit of the peace of the living, somnolent with the easement and content of prosperity, and undisturbed by rumors of far wars.

The red-coated, many-antlered buck acknowledged the lordship of the spirit of the place and dozed knee-deep in the cool, shaded pool. There seemed no flies to vex him and he was languid with rest. Sometimes his ears moved when the stream awoke and whispered; but they moved lazily, with foreknowledge that it was merely the stream grown garrulous at discovery that it had slept.

But there came a time when the buck's ears lifted and tensed with swift eagerness for sound. His head was turned down the canyon. His sensitive, quivering nostrils scented the air. His eyes could not pierce the green screen through which the stream rippled away, but to his ears came the voice of a man. It was a steady, monotonous, singsong voice. Once the buck heard the harsh clash of metal upon rock. At the sound he snorted with a sudden start that jerked him through the air from water to meadow, and his feet sank into the young velvet, while he pricked his ears and again scented the air. Then he stole across the tiny meadow, pausing once and again to listen, and faded away out of the canyon like a wraith, soft-footed and without sound.

The clash of steel-shod soles against the rocks began to be heard, and the man's voice grew louder. It was raised in a sort of chant and became distinct with nearness, so that the words could be heard:

"Tu'n around an' tu'n yo' face
Untoe them sweet hills of grace
(D' pow'rs of sin yo' am scornin'!).
Look about an' look aroun'
Fling yo' sin-pack on d' groun'
(Yo' will meet wid d' Lord in d' mornin'!)."

'A sound of scrambling accompanied the song, and the spirit of the place fled away on the heels of the red-coated buck. The green screen was burst asunder, and a man peered out at the meadow and the pool and the sloping side-hill. He was a deliberate sort of man. He took in the scene with one embracing glance, then ran his eyes over the details to verify the general impression. Then, and not until then, did he open his mouth in vivid and solemn approval:

"Smoke of life an' snakes of purgatory! Will you just look at that! Wood an' water an' grass an' a side-hill! A pocket-hunter's delight an' a cayuse's paradise! Cool green for tired eyes! Pink pills for pale people ain't in it. A secret pasture for prospectors and a resting-place for tired burros. It's just booful!"

He was a sandy-complexioned man in whose face geniality and humor seemed the salient characteristics. It was a mobile face, quick-changing to inward mood and thought. Thinking was in him a visible process. Ideas chased across his face like wind-flaws across the surface of a lake. His hair, sparse and unkempt of growth, was as indeterminate and colorless as his complexion. It would seem that all the color of his frame had gone into his eyes, for they were startlingly blue. Also, they were laughing and merry eyes, within them much of the naiveté and wonder of the child; and yet, in an unassertive way, they contained much of calm self-reliance and strength of purpose founded upon self-experience and experience of the world.

From out the screen of vines and creepers he flung ahead of him a miner's pick and shovel and gold-pan. Then he crawled out himself into the open. He was clad in faded overalls and black cotton shirt, with hobnailed brogans on his feet, and on his head a hat whose shapelessness and stains advertised the rough usage of wind and rain and sun and camp-smoke. He stood erect, seeing wide-eyed the secrecy of the scene and sensuously inhaling the warm, sweet breath of the canyon-garden through nostrils that dilated and quivered with delight. His eyes narrowed to laughing slits of blue, his face wreathed itself in joy, and his mouth curled in a smile as he cried aloud:

"Jumping dandelions and happy hollyhocks, but that smells

good to me! Talk about your attar o' roses an' cologne factories! They ain't in it!"

He had the habit of soliloquy. His quick-changing facial expressions might tell every thought and mood, but the tongue, perforce, ran hard after, repeating, like a second Boswell.

The man lay down on the lip of the pool and drank long and deep of its water. "Tastes good to me," he murmured, lifting his head and gazing across the pool at the side-hill, while he wiped his mouth with the back of his hand. The side-hill attracted his attention. Still lying on his stomach, he studied the hill formation long and carefully. It was a practised eye that traveled up the slope to the crumbling canyon-wall and back and down again to the edge of the pool. He scrambled to his feet and favored the side-hill with a second survey.

"Looks good to me," he concluded, picking up his pick and shovel and gold-pan.

He crossed the stream below the pool, stepping agilely from stone to stone. Where the side-hill touched the water he dug up a shovelful of dirt and put it into the gold-pan. He squatted down, holding the pan in his two hands, and partly immersing it in the stream. Then he imparted to the pan a deft circular motion that sent the water sluicing in and out through the dirt and gravel. The larger and the lighter particles worked to the surface, and these, by a skilful dipping movement of the pan, he spilled out and over the edge. Occasionally, to expedite matters, he rested the pan and with his fingers raked out the large pebbles and pieces of rock.

The contents of the pan diminished rapidly until only fine dirt and the smallest bits of gravel remained. At this stage he began to work very deliberately and carefully. It was fine washing, and he washed fine and finer, with a keen scrutiny and delicate and fastidious touch. At last the pan seemed empty of everything but water; but with a quick semi-circular flirt that sent the water flying over the shallow rim into the stream, he disclosed a layer of black sand on the bottom of the pan. So thin was this layer that it was like a streak of paint. He examined it closely. In the midst of it was a tiny golden speck. He dribbled a little water in over the depressed edge of the pan. With a quick flirt he sent the water sluicing across the bottom, turning the grains of black sand over and over. A second tiny golden speck rewarded his effort.

The washing had now become very fine—fine beyond all need of ordinary placer-mining. He worked the black sand, a small portion at a time, up the shallow rim of the pan. Each small portion he examined sharply, so that his eyes saw every grain of it before he allowed it to slide over the edge and away. Jealously, bit by bit, he let the black sand slip away. A golden speck, no larger than a pinpoint, appeared on the rim, and by his manipulation of the water it returned to the bottom of the pan. And in such fashion another speck was disclosed, and another. Great was his care of them. Like a shepherd he herded his flock of golden specks so that not one should be lost. At last, of the pan of dirt nothing remained but his golden herd. He counted it, and then, after all his labor, sent it flying out of the pan with one final swirl of water.

But his blue eyes were shining with desire as he rose to his feet. "Seven," he muttered aloud, asserting the sum of the specks for which he had toiled so hard and which he had so wantonly thrown away. "Seven," he repeated, with the emphasis of one trying to impress a number on his memory.

He stood still a long while, surveying the hillside. In his eyes was a curiosity, new-aroused and burning. There was an exultance about his bearing and a keenness like that of a hunting animal catching the fresh scent of game.

He moved down the stream a few steps and took a second panful of dirt.

Again came the careful washing, the jealous herding of the golden specks, and the wantonness with which he sent them flying into the stream.

"Five," he muttered, and repeated, "five."

He could not forbear another survey of the hill before filling the pan farther down the stream. His golden herds diminished. "Four, three, two, two, one," were his memory tabulations as he moved down the stream. When but one speck of gold rewarded his washing, he stopped and built a fire of dry twigs. Into this he thrust the gold-pan and burned it till it was blue-black. He held up the pan and examined it critically. Then he nodded approbation. Against such a color-background he could defy the tiniest yellow speck to elude him.

Still moving down the stream, he panned again. A single speck was his reward. A third pan contained no gold at all. Not satisfied with this, he panned three times again, taking his shovels of dirt within a foot of one another. Each pan proved empty of gold, and the fact, instead of discouraging him, seemed to give him satisfaction. His elation increased with each barren washing, until he arose, exclaiming jubilantly:

"If it ain't the real thing, may God knock off my head with sour apples!"

Returning to where he had started operations, he began to

pan up the stream. At first his golden herds increased—increased prodigiously. "Fourteen, eighteen, twenty-one, twenty-six," ran his memory tabulations. Just above the pool he struck his richest pan—thirty-five colors.

"Almost enough to save," he remarked regretfully as he allowed the water to sweep them away.

The sun climbed to the top of the sky. The man worked on. Pan by pan, he went up the stream, the tally of results steadily decreasing.

"It's just booful, the way it peters out," he exulted when a shovelful of dirt contained no more than a single speck of gold. And when no specks at all were found in several pans, he straightened up and favored the hillside with a confident glance.

"Ah, ha! Mr. Pocket!" he cried out, as though to an auditor hidden somewhere above him beneath the surface of the slope. "Ah, ha! Mr. Pocket! I'm a-comin', I'm a-comin', an' I'm shorely gwine to get yer! You heah me, Mr. Pocket? I'm gwine to get yer as shore as punkins ain't cauliflowers!"

He turned and flung a measuring glance at the sun poised above him in the azure of the cloudless sky. Then he went down the canyon, following the line of shovel-holes he had made in filling the pans. He crossed the stream below the pool and disappeared through the green screen. There was little opportunity for the spirit of the place to return with its quietude and repose, for the man's voice, raised in ragtime song, still dominated the canyon with possession.

After a time, with a greater clashing of steel-shod feet on rock, he returned. The green screen was tremendously agitated. It surged back and forth in the throes of a struggle. There was a loud grating and clanging of metal. The man's voice leaped to a higher pitch and was sharp with imperativeness. A large body plunged and panted. There was a snapping and ripping and rending, and amid a shower of falling leaves a horse burst through the screen. On its back was a pack, and from this trailed broken vines and torn creepers. The animal gazed with astonished eyes at the scene into which it had been precipitated, then dropped its head to the grass and began contentedly to graze. A second horse scrambled into view, slipping once on the mossy rocks and regaining equilibrium when its hoofs sank into the yielding surface of the meadow. It was riderless, though on its back was a high-horned Mexican saddle, scarred and discolored by long usage.

The man brought up the rear. He threw off pack and saddle, with an eye to camp location, and gave the animals their freedom to graze. He unpacked his food and got out frying-pan and coffee-pot. He gathered an armful of dry wood, and with a few stones made a place for his fire.

"My!" he said, "but I've got an appetite. I could scoff iron-filings an' horseshoe nails an' thank you kindly, ma'am, for a second helpin'."

He straightened up, and, while he reached for matches in the pocket of his overalls, his eyes traveled across the pool to the side-hill. His fingers had clutched the match-box, but they relaxed their hold and the hand came out empty. The man wavered perceptibly. He looked at his preparations for cooking and he looked at the hill.

"Guess I'll take another whack at her," he concluded, starting to cross the stream.

"They ain't no sense in it, I know," he mumbled apologetically. "But keepin' grub back an hour ain't go in' to hurt none, I reckon."

A few feet back from his first line of test-pans he started a second line. The sun dropped down the western sky, the shadows lengthened, but the man worked on. He began a third line of test-pans. He was cross-cutting the hillside, line by line, as he ascended. The center of each line produced the richest pans, while the ends came where no colors showed in the pan. And as he ascended the hillside the lines grew perceptibly shorter. The regularity with which their length diminished served to indicate that somewhere up the slope the last line would be so short as to have scarcely length at all, and that beyond could come only a point. The design was growing into an inverted "V." The converging sides of this "V" marked the boundaries of the gold-bearing dirt.

The apex of the "V" was evidently the man's goal. Often he ran his eye along the converging sides and on up the hill, trying to divine the apex, the point where the gold-bearing dirt must cease. Here resided "Mr. Pocket"—for so the man familiarly addressed the imaginary point above him on the slope, crying out:

"Come down out o' that, Mr. Pocket! Be right smart an' agreeable, an' come down!"

"All right," he would add later, in a voice resigned to determination. "All right, Mr. Pocket. It's plain to me I got to come right up an' snatch you out bald-headed. An' I'll do it! I'll do it!" he would threaten still later.

Each pan he carried down to the water to wash, and as he went higher up the hill the pans grew richer, until he began to save the gold in an empty baking powder can which he carried carelessly in his hip-pocket. So engrossed was he in his toil that he did not notice the long twilight of oncoming night. It was not until he tried vainly to see the gold colors in the bottom of the pan that he realized the passage of time. He straightened up abruptly. An expression of whimsical wonderment and awe overspread his face as he drawled:

"Gosh darn my buttons! if I didn't plumb forget dinner!"

He stumbled across the stream in the darkness and lighted his long-delayed fire. Flapjacks and bacon and warmed-over beans constituted his supper. Then he smoked a pipe by the smouldering coals, listening to the night noises and watching the moonlight stream through the canyon. After that he unrolled his bed, took off his heavy shoes, and pulled the blankets up to his chin. His face showed white in the moonlight, like the face of a corpse. But it was a corpse that knew its resurrection, for the man rose suddenly on one elbow and gazed across at his hillside.

"Good night, Mr. Pocket," he called sleepily. "Goodnight."

He slept through the early gray of morning until the direct rays of the sun smote his closed eyelids, when he awoke with a start and looked about him until he had established the continuity of his existence and identified his present self with the days previously lived.

To dress, he had merely to buckle on his shoes. He glanced at his fireplace and at his hillside, wavered, but fought down the temptation and started the fire.

"Keep yer shirt on, Bill; keep yer shirt on," he admonished himself. "What's the good of rushin'? No use in gettin' all het up an' sweaty. Mr. Pocket'll wait for you. He ain't a-runnin' away before you can get your breakfast. Now, what you want, Bill, is something fresh in yer bill o' fare. So it's up to you to go an' get it."

He cut a short pole at the water's edge and drew from one of his pockets a bit of line and a draggled fly that had once been a royal coachman.

"Mebbe they'll bite in the early morning," he muttered, as he made his first cast into the pool. And a moment later he was gleefully crying: "What'd I tell you, eh? What'd I tell you?"

He had no reel, nor any inclination to waste time, and by main strength, and swiftly, he drew out of the water a flashing ten-inch trout. Three more, caught in rapid succession, furnished his breakfast. When he came to the stepping-stones on his way to his hillside, he was struck by a sudden thought, and paused.

"I'd just better take a hike down-stream a ways," he said. "There's no tellin' who may be snoopin' around."

But he crossed over on the stones, and with a "I really oughter take that hike," the need of the precaution passed out of his mind and he fell to work.

At nightfall he straightened up. The small of his back was stiff from stooping toil, and as he put his hand behind him to soothe the protesting muscles, he said:

"Now what d'ye think of that? I clean forgot my dinner again! If I don't watch out, I'll sure be degeneratin' into a two-meal-a-day crank."

"Pockets is the hangedest things I ever see for makin' a man absent-minded," he communed that night, as he crawled into his blankets. Nor did he forget to call up the hillside, "Good night, Mr. Pocket! Good night!"

Rising with the sun, and snatching a hasty breakfast, he was early at work. A fever seemed to be growing in him, nor did the increasing richness of the test-pans allay this fever. There was a flush in his cheek other than that made by the heat of the sun, and he was oblivious to fatigue and the passage of time. When he filled a pan with dirt, he ran down the hill to wash it; nor could he forbear running up the hill again, panting and stumbling profanely, to refill the pan.

He was now a hundred yards from the water, and the inverted "V" was assuming definite proportions. The width of the pay-dirt steadily decreased, and the man extended in his mind's eye the sides of the "V" to their meeting place far up the hill. This was his goal, the apex of the "V," and he panned many times to locate it.

"Just about two yards above that manzanita bush an' a yard to the right," he finally concluded.

Then the temptation seized him. "As plain as the nose on your face," he said, as he abandoned his laborious cross-cutting and climbed to the indicated apex. He filled a pan and carried it down the hill to wash. It contained no trace of gold. He dug deep, and he dug shallow, filling and washing a dozen pans, and was unrewarded even by the tiniest golden speck. He was enraged at having yielded to the temptation, and berated himself blasphemously and pridelessly. Then he went down the hill and took up the cross-cutting.

"Slow an' certain, Bill; slow an' certain," he crooned. "Short-cuts to fortune ain't in your line, an' it's about time you know it. Get wise, Bill; get wise. Slow an' certain's the only hand you can play; so go to it, an' keep to it, too."

As the cross-cuts decreased, showing that the sides of the "V" were converging, the depth of the "V" increased. The gold-trace was dipping into the hill. It was only at thirty inches beneath the surface that he could get colors in his pan. The dirt he found at twenty-five inches from the surface, and at thirty-five inches yielded barren pans. At the base of the "V," by the water's edge, he had found the gold colors at the grass roots. The higher he went up the hill, the deeper the gold dipped. To dig a hole three feet deep in order to get one test-pan was a task of no mean magnitude; while between the man and the apex intervened an untold number of such holes to be dug. "An' there's no tellin' how much deeper it'll pitch," he sighed, in a moment's pause, while his fingers soothed his aching back.

Feverish with desire, with aching back and stiffening muscles, with pick and shovel gouging and mauling the soft brown earth, the man toiled up the hill. Before him was the smooth slope, spangled with flowers and made sweet with their breath. Behind him was devastation. It looked like some terrible eruption breaking out on the smooth skin of the hill. His slow progress was like that of a slug, befouling beauty with a monstrous trail.

Though the dipping gold-trace increased the man's work, he found consolation in the increasing richness of the pans. Twenty cents, thirty cents, fifty cents, sixty cents, were the values of the gold found in the pans, and at nightfall he washed his banner pan, which gave him a dollar's worth of gold-dust from a shovelful of dirt.

"I'll just bet it's my luck to have some inquisitive one come buttin' in here on my pasture," he mumbled sleepily that night as he pulled the blankets up to his chin.

Suddenly he sat upright. "Bill!" he called sharply. "Now, listen to me, Bill; d'ye hear! It's up to you, to-morrow mornin', to mosey round an' see what you can see. Understand? To-morrow morning, an' don't you forget it!"

He yawned and glanced across at his side-hill. "Good night, Mr. Pocket," he called.

In the morning he stole a march on the sun, for he had finished breakfast when its first rays caught him, and he was climbing the wall of the canyon where it crumbled away and gave footing. From the outlook at the top he found himself in the midst of loneliness. As far as he could see, chain after chain of mountains heaved themselves into his vision. To the east his eyes, leaping the miles between range and range and between many ranges, brought up at last against the white-peaked Sierras—the main crest, where the backbone of the Western world reared itself against the sky. To the north and south he could see more distinctly the cross-systems that broke through the main trend of the sea of mountains. To the west the ranges fell away, one behind the other, diminishing and fading into the gentle foothills that, in turn, descended into the great valley which he could not see.

And in all that mighty sweep of earth he saw no sign of man

nor of the handiwork of man—save only the torn bosom of the hillside at his feet. The man looked long and carefully. Once, far down his own canyon, he thought he saw in the air a faint hint of smoke. He looked again and decided that it was the purple haze of the hills made dark by a convolution of the canyon wall at its back.

"Hey, you, Mr. Pocket!" he called down into the canyon. "Stand out from under! I'm a-comin', Mr. Pocket! I'm a-comin'!"

The heavy brogans on the man's feet made him appear clumsy-footed, but he swung down from the giddy height as lightly and airily as a mountain goat. A rock, turning under his foot on the edge of the precipice, did not disconcert him. He seemed to know the precise time required for the turn to culminate in disaster, and in the meantime he utilized the false footing itself for the momentary earth-contact necessary to carry him on into safety. Where the earth sloped so steeply that it was impossible to stand for a second upright, the man did not hesitate. His foot pressed the impossible surface for but a fraction of the fatal second and gave him the bound that carried him onward. Again, where even the fraction of a second's footing was out of the question, he would swing his body past by a moment's hand-grip on a jutting knob of rock, a crevice, or a precariously rooted shrub. At last, with a wild leap and yell, he exchanged the face of the wall for an earth-slide and finished the descent in the midst of several tons of sliding earth and gravel.

His first pan of the morning washed out over two dollars in coarse gold. It was from the centre of the "V." To either side the diminution in the values of the pans was swift. His lines of cross-cutting holes were growing very short. The converging sides of the inverted "V" were only a few yards apart. Their meeting-point was only a few yards above him. But the pay-streak was dipping deeper and deeper into the earth. By early afternoon he was sinking the test-holes five feet before the pans could show the gold-trace.

For that matter, the gold-trace had become something more than a trace; it was a placer mine in itself, and the man resolved to come back after he had found the pocket and work over the ground. But the increasing richness of the pans began to worry him. By late afternoon the worth of the pans had grown to three and four dollars. The man scratched his head perplexedly and looked a few feet up the hill at the manzanita bush that marked approximately the apex of the "V." He nodded his head and said oracularly:

"It's one o' two things, Bill: one o' two things. Either Mr. Pocket's spilled himself all out an' down the hill, or else Mr. Pocket's so rich you maybe won't be able to carry him all away with you. And that'd be an awful shame, wouldn't it, now?" He chuckled at contemplation of so pleasant a dilemma.

Nightfall found him by the edge of the stream, his eyes wrestling with the gathering darkness over the washing of a five-dollar pan.

"Wisht I had an electric light to go on working," he said.

He found sleep difficult that night. Many times he composed himself and closed his eyes for slumber to overtake him; but his blood pounded with too strong desire, and as many times his eyes opened and he murmured wearily, "Wisht it was sun-up."

Sleep came to him in the end, but his eyes were open with the first paling of the stars, and the gray of dawn caught him with breakfast finished and climbing the hillside in the direction of the secret abiding-place of Mr. Pocket.

The first cross-cut the man made, there was space for only three holes, so narrow had become the pay-streak and so close was he to the fountainhead of the golden stream he had been following for four days.

"Be ca'm, Bill; be ca'm," he admonished himself, as he broke ground for the final hole where the sides of the "V" had at last come together in a point.

"I've got the almighty cinch on you, Mr. Pocket, an' you can't lose me," he said many times as he sank the hole deeper and deeper.

Four feet, five feet, six feet, he dug his way down into the earth. The digging grew harder. His pick grated on broken rock. He examined the rock. "Rotten quartz," was his conclusion as, with the shovel, he cleared the bottom of the hole of loose dirt. He attacked the crumbling quartz with the pick, bursting the disintegrating rock asunder with every stroke.

He thrust his shovel into the loose mass. His eye caught a gleam of yellow. He dropped the shovel and squatted suddenly on his heels. As a farmer rubs the clinging earth from fresh-dug potatoes, so the man, a piece of rotten quartz held in both hands, rubbed the dirt away.

"Sufferin' Sardanopolis!" he cried. "Lumps an' chunks of it! Lumps an' chunks of it!"

It was only half rock he held in his hand. The other half was virgin gold. He dropped it into his pan and examined another piece. Little yellow was to be seen, but with his strong fingers he crumbled the rotten quartz away till both hands were filled with glowing yellow. He rubbed the dirt away from fragment after fragment, tossing them into the gold-pan. It was a treasure-hole. So much had the quartz rotted away that there was less of it than there was of gold. Now and again he found a piece to which no rock clung—a piece that was all gold. A chunk, where the pick had laid open the heart of the gold, glittered like a handful of yellow jewels, and he cocked his head at it and slowly turned it around and over to observe the rich play of the light upon it.

"Talk about yer Too Much Gold diggin's!" the man snorted contemptuously. "Why, this diggin' 'd make it look like thirty cents. This diggin' is All Gold. An' right here an' now I name this yere canyon 'All Gold Canyon,' b' gosh!"

Still squatting on his heels, he continued examining the fragments and tossing them into the pan. Suddenly there came to him a premonition of danger. It seemed a shadow had fallen upon him. But there was no shadow. His heart had given a great jump up into his throat and was choking him. Then his blood slowly chilled and he felt the sweat of his shirt cold against his flesh.

He did not spring up nor look around. He did not move. He was considering the nature of the premonition he had received, trying to locate the source of the mysterious force that had warned him, striving to sense the imperative presence of the unseen thing that threatened him. There is an aura of things hostile, made manifest by messengers too refined for the senses to know; and this aura he felt, but knew not how he felt it. His was the feeling as when a cloud passes over the sun. It seemed that between him and life had passed something dark and smothering and menacing; a gloom, as it were, that swallowed up life and made for death—his death.

Every force of his being impelled him to spring up and confront the unseen danger, but his soul dominated the panic, and he remained squatting on his heels, in his hands a chunk of gold. He did not dare to look around, but he knew by now that there was something behind him and above him. He made believe to be interested in the gold in his hand. He examined it critically, turned it over and over, and rubbed the dirt from it. And all the time he knew that something behind him was looking at the gold over his shoulder.

Still feigning interest in the chunk of gold in his hand, he listened intently and he heard the breathing of the thing behind him. His eyes searched the ground in front of him for a weapon, but they saw only the uprooted gold, worthless to him now in his extremity. There was his pick, a handy weapon on occasion; but this was not such an occasion. The man realized his predicament. He was in a narrow hole that was seven feet deep. His head did not come to the surface of the ground. He was in a trap.

He remained squatting on his heels. He was quite cool and

collected; but his mind, considering every factor, showed him only his helplessness. He continued rubbing the dirt from the quartz fragments and throwing the gold into the pan. There was nothing else for him to do. Yet he knew that he would have to rise up, sooner or later, and face the danger that breathed at his back. The minutes passed, and with the passage of each minute he knew that by so much he was nearer the time when he must stand up, or else—and his wet shirt went cold against his flesh again at the thought—or else he might receive death as he stooped there over his treasure.

Still he squatted on his heels, rubbing dirt from gold and debating in just what manner he should rise up. He might rise up with a rush and claw his way out of the hole to meet whatever threatened on the even footing above ground. Or he might rise up slowly and carelessly, and feign casually to discover the thing that breathed at his back. His instinct and every fighting fibre of his body favored the mad, clawing rush to the surface. His intellect, and the craft thereof, favored the slow and cautious meeting with the thing that menaced and which he could not see. And while he debated, a loud, crashing noise burst on his ear. At the same instant he received a stunning blow on the left side of the back, and from the point of impact felt a rush of flame through his flesh. He sprang up in the air, but halfway to his feet collapsed. His body crumpled in like a leaf withered in sudden heat, and he came down, his chest across his pan of gold, his face in the dirt and rock, his legs tangled and twisted because of the restricted space at the bottom of the hole. His legs twitched convulsively several times. His body was shaken as with a mighty ague. There was a slow expansion of the lungs, accompanied by a deep sigh. Then the air was slowly, very slowly, exhaled, and his body as slowly flattened itself down into inertness.

Above, revolver in hand, a man was peering down over the edge of the hole. He peered for a long time at the prone and motionless body beneath him. After a while the stranger sat down on the edge of the hole so that he could see into it, and rested the revolver on his knee. Reaching his hand into a pocket, he drew out a wisp of brown paper. Into this he dropped a few crumbs of tobacco. The combination became a cigarette, brown and squat, with the ends turned in. Not once did he take his eyes from the body at the bottom of the hole. He lighted the cigarette and drew its smoke into his lungs with a caressing intake of the breath. He smoked slowly. Once the cigarette went out and he relighted it. And all the while he studied the body beneath him.

In the end he tossed the cigarette stub away and rose to his feet. He moved to the edge of the hole. Spanning it, a hand resting on each edge, and with the revolver still in the right hand, he muscled his body down into the hole. While his feet were yet a yard from the bottom he released his hands and dropped down.

At the instant his feet struck bottom he saw the pocket-miner's arm leap out, and his own legs knew a swift, jerking grip that overthrew him. In the nature of the jump his revolver hand was above his head. Swiftly as the grip had flashed about his legs, just as swiftly he brought the revolver down. He was still in the air, his fall in process of completion, when he pulled the trigger. The explosion was deafening in the confined space. The smoke filled the hole so that he could see nothing. He struck the bottom on his back, and like a cat's the pocket-miner's body was on top of him. Even as the miner's body passed on top, the stranger crooked in his right arm to fire; and even in that instant the miner, with a quick thrust of elbow, struck his wrist. The muzzle was thrown up and the bullet thudded into the dirt of the side of the hole.

The next instant the stranger felt the miner's hand grip his wrist. The struggle was now for the revolver. Each man strove to turn it against the other's body. The smoke in the hole was clearing. The stranger, lying on his back, was beginning to see dimly. But suddenly he was blinded by a handful of dirt deliberately flung into his eyes by his antagonist. In that moment of shock his grip on the revolver was broken. In the next moment he felt a smashing darkness descend upon his brain, and in the midst of the darkness even the darkness ceased.

But the pocket-miner fired again and again, until the revolver was empty. Then he tossed it from him and, breathing heavily, sat down on the dead man's legs.

The miner was sobbing and struggling for breath. "Measly skunk!" he panted; "a-campin' on my trail an' lettin' me do the work, an' then shootin' me in the back!"

He was half crying from anger and exhaustion. He peered at the face of the dead man. It was sprinkled with loose dirt and gravel, and it was difficult to distinguish the features.

"Never laid eyes on him before," the miner concluded his scrutiny. "Just a common an' ordinary thief, hang him! An' he shot me in the back! He shot me in the back!"

He opened his shirt and felt himself, front and back, on his left side.

"Went clean through, and no harm done!" he cried jubilantly. "I'll bet he aimed all right all right; but he drew the gun over when he pulled the trigger—the cur! But I fixed 'm! Oh, I fixed 'm!"

His fingers were investigating the bullet-hole in his side, and a shade of regret passed over his face. "It's goin' to be stiffer'n hell," he said. "An' it's up to me to get mended an' get out o'here."

He crawled out of the hole and went down the hill to his camp. Half an hour later he returned, leading his pack-horse. His open shirt disclosed the rude bandages with which he had dressed his wound. He was slow and awkward with his left-hand movements, but that did not prevent his using the arm.

The bight of the pack-rope under the dead man's shoulders enabled him to heave the body out of the hole. Then he set to work gathering up his gold. He worked steadily for several hours, pausing often to rest his stiffening shoulder and to exclaim:

"He shot me in the back, the measly skunk! He shot me in the back!"

When his treasure was quite cleaned up and wrapped securely into a number of blanket-covered parcels, he made an estimate of its value.

"Four hundred pounds, or I'm a Hottentot," he concluded. "Say two hundred in quartz an' dirt—that leaves two hundred pounds of gold. Bill! Wake up! Two hundred pounds of gold! Forty thousand dollars! An' it's yourn—all yourn!"

He scratched his head delightedly and his fingers blundered into an unfamiliar groove. They quested along it for several inches. It was a crease through his scalp where the second bullet had ploughed.

He walked angrily over to the dead man.

"You would, would you!" he bullied. "You would, eh? Well, I fixed you good an' plenty, an' I'll give you decent burial, too. That's more'n you'd have done for me."

He dragged the body to the edge of the hole and toppled it in. It struck the bottom with a dull crash, on its side, the face twisted up to the light. The miner peered down at it.

"An' you shot me in the back!" he said accusingly.

With pick and shovel he filled the hole. Then he loaded the gold on his horse. It was too great a load for the animal, and when he had gained his camp he transferred part of it to his saddle-horse. Even so, he was compelled to abandon a portion of his outfit—pick and shovel and gold-pan, extra food and cooking utensils, and divers odds and ends.

The sun was at the zenith when the man forced the horses at the screen of vines and creepers. To climb the huge boulders the animals were compelled to uprear and struggle blindly through the tangled mass of vegetation. Once the saddle-horse fell heavily and the man removed the pack to get the animal on its feet. After it started on its way again the man thrust his head out from among the leaves and peered up at the hillside.

"The measly skunk!" he said, and disappeared.

There was a ripping and tearing of vines and boughs. The trees surged back and forth, marking the passage of the animals through the midst of them. There was a clashing of steel-shod hoofs on stone, and now and again a sharp cry of command. Then the voice of the man was raised in song:—

"Tu'n around an' tu'n yo' face
Untoe them sweet hills of grace
(D' pow'rs of sin yo' am scornin'!).
Look about an' look aroun'
Fling yo' sin-pack on d' groun'
(Yo'-will meet wid d' Lord in d' mornin'!)."

The song grew faint and fainter, and through the silence crept back the spirit of the place. The stream once more drowsed and whispered; the hum of the mountain bees rose sleepily. Down through the perfume-weighted air fluttered the snowy fluffs of the cottonwoods. The butterflies drifted in and out among the trees, and over all blazed the quiet sunshine. Only remained the hoof-marks in the meadow and the torn hillside to mark the boisterous trail of the life that had broken the peace of the place and passed on.

THE STORY OF KEESH

Keesh lived long ago on the rim of the polar sea, was head man of his village through many and prosperous years, and died full of honors with his name on the lips of men. So long ago did he live that only the old men remember his name, his name and the tale, which they got from the old men before them, and which the old men to come will tell to their children and their children's children down to the end of time. And the winter darkness, when the north gales make their long sweep across the ice-pack, and the air is filled with flying white, and no man may venture forth, is the chosen time for the telling of how Keesh, from the poorest igloo in the village, rose to power and place over them all.

He was a bright boy, so the tale runs, healthy and strong, and he had seen thirteen suns, in their way of reckoning time. For each winter the sun leaves the land in darkness, and the next year a new sun returns so that they may be warm again and look upon one another's faces. The father of Keesh had been a very brave man, but he had met his death in a time of famine, when he sought to save the lives of his people by taking the life of a great polar bear. In his eagerness he came to close grapples with the bear, and his bones were crushed; but the bear had much meat on him and the people were saved. Keesh was his only son, and after that Keesh lived alone with his mother. But the people are prone to forget, and they forgot the deed of his father; and he being but a boy, and his mother only a woman, they, too, were swiftly forgotten, and ere long came to live in the meanest of all the igloos.

It was at a council, one night, in the big igloo of Klosh-Kwan, the chief, that Keesh showed the blood that ran in his veins and the manhood that stiffened his back. With the dignity of an elder, he rose to his feet, and waited for silence amid the babble of voices.

"It is true that meat be apportioned me and mine," he said. "But it is ofttimes old and tough, this meat, and, moreover, it has an unusual quantity of bones."

The hunters, grizzled and gray, and lusty and young, were aghast. The like had never been known before. A child, that talked like a grown man, and said harsh things to their very faces!

But steadily and with seriousness, Keesh went on. "For that I know my father, Bok, was a great hunter, I speak these words. It is said that Bok brought home more meat than any of the two best hunters, that with his own hands he attended to the division of it, that with his own eyes he saw to it that the least old woman and the least old man received fair share."

"Na! Na!" the men cried. "Put the child out!" "Send him off to bed!" "He is no man that he should talk to men and gray-beards!"

He waited calmly till the uproar died down.

"Thou hast a wife, Ugh-Gluk," he said, "and for her dost thou speak. And thou, too, Massuk, a mother also, and for them dost thou speak. My mother has no one, save me; wherefore I speak. As I say, though Bok be dead because he hunted over-keenly, it is just that I, who am his son, and that Ikeega, who is my mother and was his wife, should have meat in plenty so long as there be meat in plenty in the tribe. I, Keesh, the son of Bok, have spoken."

He sat down, his ears keenly alert to the flood of protest and indignation his words had created.

"That a boy should speak in council!" old Ugh-Gluk was mumbling.

"Shall the babes in arms tell us men the things we shall do?" Massuk demanded in a loud voice. "Am I a man that I should be made a mock by every child that cries for meat?"

The anger boiled a white heat. They ordered him to bed, threatened that he should have no meat at all, and promised him sore beatings for his presumption. Keesh's eyes began to flash, and the blood to pound darkly under his skin. In the midst of the abuse he sprang to his feet.

"Hear me, ye men!" he cried. "Never shall I speak in the council again, never again till the men come to me and say, 'It is well, Keesh, that thou shouldst speak, it is well and it is our wish.' Take this now, ye men, for my last word. Bok, my father, was a great hunter. I too, his son, shall go and hunt the meat that I eat. And be it known, now, that the division of that which I kill shall be fair. And no widow nor weak one shall cry in the night because there is no meat, when the strong men are groaning in great pain for that they have eaten overmuch. And in the days to come there shall be shame upon the strong men who have eaten overmuch. I, Keesh, have said it!"

Jeers and scornful laughter followed him out of the igloo, but his jaw was set and he went his way, looking neither to right nor left.

The next day he went forth along the shoreline where the ice and the land met together. Those who saw him go noted that he carried his bow, with a goodly supply of bone-barbed arrows, and that across his shoulder was his father's big hunting-spear. And there was laughter, and much talk, at the event. It was an unprecedented occurrence. Never did boys of his tender age go forth to hunt, much less to hunt alone. Also were there shaking of heads and prophetic mutterings, and the women looked pityingly at Ikeega, and her face was grave and sad.

"He will be back ere long," they said cheeringly.

"Let him go; it will teach him a lesson," the hunters said. "And he will come back shortly, and he will be meek and soft of speech in the days to follow."

But a day passed, and a second, and on the third a wild gale blew, and there was no Keesh. Ikeega tore her hair and put soot of the seal-oil on her face in token of her grief; and the women assailed the men with bitter words in that they had mistreated the boy and sent him to his death; and the men made no answer, preparing to go in search of the body when the storm abated.

Early next morning, however, Keesh strode into the village. But he came not shamefacedly. Across his shoulders he bore a burden of fresh-killed meat. And there was importance in his step and arrogance in his speech.

"Go, ye men, with the dogs and sledges, and take my trail for the better part of a day's travel," he said. "There is much meat on the ice—a she-bear and two half-grown cubs."

Ikeega was overcome with joy, but he received her demonstrations in manlike fashion, saying: "Come, Ikeega, let us eat. And after that I shall sleep, for I am weary."

And he passed into their igloo and ate profoundly, and after that slept for twenty running hours.

There was much doubt at first, much doubt and discussion. The killing of a polar bear is very dangerous, but thrice dangerous is it, and three times thrice, to kill a mother bear with her cubs. The men could not bring themselves to believe that the boy Keesh, single-handed, had accomplished so great a marvel. But the women spoke of the fresh-killed meat he had brought on his back, and this was an overwhelming argument against their unbelief. So they finally departed, grumbling greatly that in all probability, if the thing were so, he had neglected to cut up the carcasses. Now in the north it is very necessary that this should be done as soon as a kill is made. If not, the meat freezes so solidly as to turn the edge of the sharpest knife, and a three-hundred-pound bear, frozen stiff, is no easy thing to put upon a sled and haul over the rough ice. But arrived at the spot, they found not only the kill which they had doubted, but that Keesh had quartered the beasts in true hunter fashion, and removed the entrails.

Thus began the mystery of Keesh, a mystery that deepened and deepened with the passing of the days. His very next trip he killed a young bear, nearly full-grown, and on the trip following, a large male bear and his mate. He was ordinarily gone from three to four days, though it was nothing unusual for him to stay away a week at a time on the ice-field. Always he declined company on these expeditions, and the people marveled. "How does he do it?" they demanded of one another. "Never does he take a dog with him, and dogs are of such great help, too."

"Why dost thou hunt only bear?" Klosh-Kwan once ventured to ask.

And Keesh made fitting answer. "It is well known that there is more meat on the bear," he said.

But there was also talk of witchcraft in the village. "He hunts with evil spirits," some of the people contended, "wherefore his hunting is rewarded. How else can it be, save that he hunts with evil spirits?"

"Mayhap they be not evil, but good, these spirits," others said. "It is known that his father was a mighty hunter. May not his father hunt with him so that he may attain excellence and patience and understanding? Who knows?"

None the less, his success continued, and the less skilful hunters were often kept busy hauling in his meat. And in the division of it he was just. As his father had done before him, he saw to it that the least old woman and the last old man received a fair portion, keeping no more for himself than his needs required. And because of this, and of his merit as a hunter, he was looked upon with respect, and even awe; and there was talk of making him chief after old Klosh-Kwan. Because of the things he had done, they looked for him to appear again in the council, but he never came, and they were ashamed to ask.

"I am minded to build me an igloo," he said one day to Klosh-Kwan and a number of the hunters. "It shall be a large igloo, wherein Ikeega and I can dwell in comfort."

"Ay," they nodded gravely.

"But I have no time. My business is hunting, and it takes all my time. So it is but just that the men and women of the village who eat my meat should build me my igloo."

And the igloo was built accordingly, on a generous scale which exceeded even the dwelling of Klosh-Kwan. Keesh and his mother moved into it, and it was the first prosperity she had enjoyed since the death of Bok. Nor was material prosperity alone hers, for, because of her wonderful son and the position he had given her, she came to be looked upon as the first woman in all the village; and the women were given to visiting her, to asking her advice, and to quoting her wisdom when arguments arose among themselves or with the men.

But it was the mystery of Keesh's marvelous hunting that took chief place in all their minds. And one day Ugh-Gluk taxed him with witchcraft to his face.

"It is charged," Ugh-Gluk said ominously, "that thou dealest with evil spirits, wherefore thy hunting is rewarded."

"Is not the meat good?" Keesh made answer. "Has one in the village yet to fall sick from the eating of it! How dost thou know that witchcraft be concerned? Or dost thou guess, in the dark, merely because of the envy that consumes thee?"

And Ugh-Gluk withdrew discomfited, the women laughing at him as he walked away. But in the council one night, after long deliberation, it was determined to put spies on his track when he went forth to hunt, so that his methods might be learned. So, on his next trip, Bim and Bawn, two young men, and of hunters the craftiest, followed after him, taking care not to be seen. After five days they returned, their eyes bulging and their tongues a-tremble to tell what they had seen. The council was hastily called in Klosh-Kwan's dwelling, and Bim took up the tale.

"Brothers! As commanded, we journeyed on the trail of Keesh, and cunningly we journeyed, so that he might not know. And midway of the first day he picked up with a great he-bear. It was a very great bear."

"None greater," Bawn corroborated, and went on himself. "Yet was the bear not inclined to fight, for he turned away and made off slowly over the ice. This we saw from the rocks of the shore, and the bear came toward us, and after him came Keesh, very much unafraid. And he shouted harsh words after the bear, and waved his arms about, and made much noise. Then did the bear grow angry, and rise up on his hind legs, and growl. But Keesh walked right up to the bear."

"Ay," Bim continued the story. "Right up to the bear Keesh walked. And the bear took after him, and Keesh ran away. But as he ran he dropped a little round ball on the ice. And the bear stopped and smelled of it, and then swallowed it up. And Keesh continued to run away and drop little round balls, and the bear continued to swallow them up."

Exclamations and cries of doubt were being made, and Ugh-Gluk expressed open unbelief.

"With our own eyes we saw it," Bim affirmed.

And Bawn—"Ay, with our own eyes. And this continued until the bear stood suddenly upright and cried aloud in pain, and thrashed his forepaws madly about. And Keesh continued to make off over the ice to a safe distance. But the bear gave him no notice, being occupied with the misfortune the little round balls had wrought within him."

"Ay, within him," Bim interrupted. "For he did claw at himself, and leap about over the ice like a playful puppy, save from the way he growled and squealed it was plain it was not play but pain. Never did I see such a sight!"

"Nay, never was such a sight seen," Bawn took up the strain. "And furthermore, it was such a large bear."

"Witchcraft," Ugh-Gluk suggested.

"I know not," Bawn replied. "I tell only of what my eyes beheld. And after a while the bear grew weak and tired, for he was very heavy and he had jumped about with exceeding violence, and he went off along the shore-ice, shaking his head slowly from side to side and sitting down ever and again to squeal and cry. And Keesh followed after the bear, and we followed after Keesh, and for that day and three days more we followed. The bear grew weak, and never ceased crying from his pain."

"It was a charm!" Ugh-Gluk exclaimed. "Surely it was a charm!"

"It may well be."

And Bim relieved Bawn. "The bear wandered, now this way and now that, doubling back and forth and crossing his trail in circles, so that at the end he was near where Keesh had first come upon him. By this time he was quite sick, the bear, and could crawl no farther, so Keesh came up close and speared him to death."

"And then?" Klosh-Kwan demanded.

"Then we left Keesh skinning the bear, and came running that the news of the killing might be told."

And in the afternoon of that day the women hauled in the meat of the bear while the men sat in council assembled. When Keesh arrived a messenger was sent to him, bidding him come to the council. But he sent reply, saying that he was hungry and tired; also that his igloo was large and comfortable and could hold many men.

And curiosity was so strong on the men that the whole council, Klosh-Kwan to the fore, rose up and went to the igloo of Keesh. He was eating, but he received them with respect and seated them according to their rank. Ikeega was proud and embarrassed by turns, but Keesh was quite composed.

Klosh-Kwan recited the information brought by Bim and Bawn, and at its close said in a stern voice: "So explanation is wanted, O Keesh, of thy manner of hunting. Is there witchcraft in it?"

Keesh looked up and smiled. "Nay, O Klosh-Kwan. It is not for a boy to know aught of witches, and of witches I know nothing. I have but devised a means whereby I may kill the ice-bear with ease, that is all. It be headcraft, not witchcraft."

"And may any man?"

"Any man."

There was a long silence. The men looked in one another's faces, and Keesh went on eating.

"And ... and ... and wilt thou tell us, O Keesh?" Klosh-Kwan finally asked in a tremulous voice.

"Yea, I will tell thee." Keesh finished sucking a marrow-bone and rose to his feet. "It is quite simple. Behold!"

He picked up a thin strip of whalebone and showed it to them. The ends were sharp as needle-points. The strip he coiled carefully, till it disappeared in his hand. Then, suddenly releasing it, it sprang straight again. He picked up a piece of blubber.

"So," he said, "one takes a small chunk of blubber, thus, and thus makes it hollow. Then into the hollow goes the whalebone, so, tightly coiled, and another piece of blubber is fitted over the whalebone. After that it is put outside where it freezes into a little round ball. The bear swallows the little round ball, the blubber melts, the whalebone with its sharp ends stands out straight, the bear gets sick, and when the bear is very sick, why, you kill him with a spear. It is quite simple."

And Ugh-Gluk said "Oh!" and Klosh-Kwan said "Ah!" And each said something after his own manner, and all understood.

And this is the story of Keesh, who lived long ago on the rim of the polar sea. Because he exercised headcraft and not witchcraft, he rose from the meanest igloo to be head man of his village, and through all the years that he lived, it is related, his tribe was prosperous, and neither widow nor weak one cried aloud in the night because there was no meat.

NAM-BOK THE UNVERACIOUS

"A Bidarka, is it not so! Look! a bidarka, and one man who drives clumsily with a paddle!"

Old Bask-Wah-Wan rose to her knees, trembling with weakness and eagerness, and gazed out over the sea.

"Nam-Bok was ever clumsy at the paddle," she maundered reminiscently, shading the sun from her eyes and staring across the silver-spilled water. "Nam-Bok was ever clumsy. I remember...."

But the women and children laughed loudly, and there was a gentle mockery in their laughter, and her voice dwindled till her lips moved without sound.

Koogah lifted his grizzled head from his bone-carving and followed the path of her eyes. Except when wide yawns took it off its course, a bidarka was heading in for the beach. Its occupant was paddling with more strength than dexterity, and made his approach along the zigzag line of most resistance. Koogah's head dropped to his work again, and on the ivory tusk between his knees he scratched the dorsal fin of a fish the like of which never swam in the sea.

"It is doubtless the man from the next village," he said finally, "come to consult with me about the marking of things on bone. And the man is a clumsy man. He will never know how."

"It is Nam-Bok," old Bask-Wah-Wan repeated. "Should I not know my son!" she demanded shrilly. "I say, and I say again, it is Nam-Bok."

"And so thou hast said these many summers," one of the women chided softly. "Ever when the ice passed out of the sea hast thou sat and watched through the long day, saying at each chance canoe, 'This is Nam-Bok.' Nam-Bok is dead, O Bask-Wah-Wan, and the dead do not come back. It cannot be that the dead come back."

"Nam-Bok!" the old woman cried, so loud and clear that the whole village was startled and looked at her.

She struggled to her feet and tottered down the sand. She stumbled over a baby lying in the sun, and the mother hushed its crying and hurled harsh words after the old woman, who took no notice. The children ran down the beach in advance of her, and as the man in the bidarka drew closer, nearly capsizing with one of his ill-directed strokes, the women followed. Koogah dropped his walrus tusk and went also, leaning heavily upon his staff, and after him loitered the men in twos and threes.

The bidarka turned broadside and the ripple of surf threatened to swamp it, only a naked boy ran into the water and pulled the bow high up on the sand. The man stood up and sent a questing glance along the line of villagers. A rainbow sweater, dirty and the worse for wear, clung loosely to his broad shoulders, and a red cotton handkerchief was knotted in sailor fashion about his throat. A fisherman's tam-o'-shanter on his close-clipped head, and dungaree trousers and heavy brogans completed his outfit.

But he was none the less a striking personage to these simple fisherfolk of the great Yukon Delta, who, all their lives, had stared out on Bering Sea and in that time seen but two white men,—the census enumerator and a lost Jesuit priest. They were a poor people, with neither gold in the ground nor valuable furs in hand, so the whites had passed them afar. Also, the Yukon, through the thousands of years, had shoaled that portion of the sea with the detritus of Alaska till vessels grounded out of sight of land. So the sodden coast, with its long inside reaches and huge mud-land archipelagoes, was avoided by the ships of men, and the fisherfolk knew not that such things were.

Koogah, the Bone-Scratcher, retreated backward in sudden haste, tripping over his staff and falling to the ground. "Nam-Bok!" he cried, as he scrambled wildly for footing. "Nam-Bok, who was blown off to sea, come back!"

The men and women shrank away, and the children scuttled off between their legs. Only Opee-Kwan was brave, as befitted the head man of the village. He strode forward and gazed long and earnestly at the newcomer.

"It is Nam-Bok," he said at last, and at the conviction in his voice the women wailed apprehensively and drew farther away.

The lips of the stranger moved indecisively, and his brown throat writhed and wrestled with unspoken words.

"La, la, it is Nam-Bok," Bask-Wah-Wan croaked, peering up into his face. "Ever did I say Nam-Bok would come back."

"Ay, it is Nam-Bok come back." This time it was Nam-Bok himself who spoke, putting a leg over the side of the bidarka and standing with one foot afloat and one ashore. Again his throat writhed and wrestled as he grappled after forgotten words. And when the words came forth they were strange of sound and a spluttering of the lips accompanied the gutturals. "Greetings, O brothers," he said, "brothers of old time before I went away with the off-shore wind."

He stepped out with both feet on the sand, and Opee-Kwan waved him back.

"Thou art dead, Nam-Bok," he said.

Nam-Bok laughed. "I am fat."

"Dead men are not fat," Opee-Kwan confessed. "Thou hast fared well, but it is strange. No man may mate with the off-shore wind and come back on the heels of the years."

"I have come back," Nam-Bok answered simply.

"Mayhap thou art a shadow, then, a passing shadow of the Nam-Bok that was. Shadows come back."

"I am hungry. Shadows do not eat."

But Opee-Kwan doubted, and brushed his hand across his brow in sore puzzlement. Nam-Bok was likewise puzzled, and as he looked up and down the line found no welcome in the eyes of the fisherfolk. The men and women whispered together. The children stole timidly back among their elders, and bristling dogs fawned up to him and sniffed suspiciously.

"I bore thee, Nam-Bok, and I gave thee suck when thou wast little," Bask-Wah-Wan whimpered, drawing closer; "and shadow though thou be, or no shadow, I will give thee to eat now."

Nam-Bok made to come to her, but a growl of fear and menace warned him back. He said something angrily in a strange tongue, and added, "No shadow am I, but a man."

"Who may know concerning the things of mystery?" Opee-Kwan demanded, half of himself and half of his tribespeople. "We are, and in a breath we are not. If the man may become shadow, may not the shadow become man? Nam-Bok was, but is not. This we know, but we do not know if this be Nam-Bok or the shadow of Nam-Bok."

Nam-Bok cleared his throat and made answer. "In the old time long ago, thy father's father, Opee-Kwan, went away and came back on the heels of the years. Nor was a place by the fire denied him. It is said ..." He paused significantly, and they hung on his utterance. "It is said," he repeated, driving his point home with deliberation, "that Sipsip, his klooch, bore him two sons after he came back."

"But he had no doings with the off-shore wind," Opee-Kwan retorted. "He went away into the heart of the land, and it is in the nature of things that a man may go on and on into the land."

"And likewise the sea. But that is neither here nor there. It is said ... that thy father's father told strange tales of the things he saw."

"Ay, strange tales he told."

"I, too, have strange tales to tell," Nam-Bok stated insidiously. And, as they wavered, "And presents likewise."

He pulled from the bidarka a shawl, marvelous of texture and color, and flung it about his mother's shoulders. The women voiced a collective sigh of admiration, and old Bask-Wah-Wan ruffled the gay material and patted it and crooned in childish joy.

"He has tales to tell," Koogah muttered. "And presents," a woman seconded.

And Opee-Kwan knew that his people were eager, and further, he was aware himself of an itching curiosity concerning those untold tales. "The fishing has been good," he said judiciously, "and we have oil in plenty. So come, Nam-Bok, let us feast."

Two of the men hoisted the bidarka on their shoulders and carried it up to the fire. Nam-Bok walked by the side of Opee-Kwan, and the villagers followed after, save those of the women who lingered a moment to lay caressing fingers on the shawl.

There was little talk while the feast went on, though many and curious were the glances stolen at the son of Bask-Wah-Wan. This embarrassed him—not because he was modest of spirit, however, but for the fact that the stench of the seal-oil had robbed him of his appetite, and that he keenly desired to conceal his feelings on the subject.

"Eat; thou art hungry," Opee-Kwan commanded, and Nam-Bok shut both his eyes and shoved his fist into the big pot of putrid fish.

"La la, be not ashamed. The seal were many this year, and strong men are ever hungry." And Bask-Wah-Wan sopped a particularly offensive chunk of salmon into the oil and passed it fondly and dripping to her son.

In despair, when premonitory symptoms warned him that his stomach was not so strong as of old, he filled his pipe and struck up a smoke. The people fed on noisily and watched. Few of them could boast of intimate acquaintance with the precious weed, though now and again small quantities and abominable qualities were obtained in trade from the Eskimos to the northward. Koogah, sitting next to him, indicated that he was not averse to taking a draw, and between two mouthfuls, with the oil thick on his lips, sucked away at the amber stem. And thereupon Nam-Bok held his stomach with a shaky hand and declined the proffered return. Koogah could keep the pipe, he said, for he had intended so to honor him from the first. And the people licked their fingers and approved of his liberality.

Opee-Kwan rose to his feet. "And now, O Nam-Bok, the feast is ended, and we would listen concerning the strange things you have seen."

The fisherfolk applauded with their hands, and gathering

about them their work, prepared to listen. The men were busy fashioning spears and carving on ivory, while the women scraped the fat from the hides of the hair seal and made them pliable or sewed muclucs with threads of sinew. Nam-Bok's eyes roved over the scene, but there was not the charm about it that his recollection had warranted him to expect. During the years of his wandering he had looked forward to just this scene, and now that it had come he was disappointed. It was a bare and meagre life, he deemed, and not to be compared to the one to which he had become used. Still, he would open their eyes a bit, and his own eyes sparkled at the thought.

"Brothers," he began, with the smug complacency of a man about to relate the big things he has done, "it was late summer of many summers back, with much such weather as this promises to be, when I went away. You all remember the day, when the gulls flew low, and the wind blew strong from the land, and I could not hold my bidarka against it. I tied the covering of the bidarka about me so that no water could get in, and all of the night I fought with the storm. And in the morning there was no land,—only the sea,—and the off-shore wind held me close in its arms and bore me along. Three such nights whitened into dawn and showed me no land, and the off-shore wind would not let me go.

"And when the fourth day came, I was as a madman. I could not dip my paddle for want of food; and my head went round and round, what of the thirst that was upon me. But the sea was no longer angry, and the soft south wind was blowing, and as I looked about me I saw a sight that made me think I was indeed mad."

Nam-Bok paused to pick away a sliver of salmon lodged between his teeth, and the men and women, with idle hands and heads craned forward, waited.

"It was a canoe, a big canoe. If all the canoes I have ever seen were made into one canoe, it would not be so large."

There were exclamations of doubt, and Koogah, whose years were many, shook his head.

"If each bidarka were as a grain of sand," Nam-Bok defiantly continued, "and if there were as many bidarkas as there be grains of sand in this beach, still would they not make so big a canoe as this I saw on the morning of the fourth day. It was a very big canoe, and it was called a schooner. I saw this thing of wonder, this great schooner, coming after me, and on it I saw men——"

"Hold, O Nam-Bok!" Opee-Kwan broke in. "What manner of men were they?—big men?"

"Nay, mere men like you and me."

"Did the big canoe come fast?"

"Ay."

"The sides were tall, the men short." Opee-Kwan stated the premises with conviction. "And did these men dip with long paddles?"

Nam-Bok grinned. "There were no paddles," he said.

Mouths remained open, and a long silence dropped down. Ope-Kwan borrowed Koogah's pipe for a couple of contemplative sucks. One of the younger women giggled nervously and drew upon herself angry eyes.

"There were no paddles?" Opee-Kwan asked softly, returning the pipe.

"The south wind was behind," Nam-Bok explained.

"But the wind drift is slow."

"The schooner had wings—thus." He sketched a diagram of masts and sails in the sand, and the men crowded around and studied it. The wind was blowing briskly, and for more graphic elucidation he seized the corners of his mother's shawl and spread them out till it bellied like a sail. Bask Wah-Wan scolded and struggled, but was blown down the breach for a score of feet and left breathless and stranded in a heap of driftwood. The men uttered sage grunts of comprehension, but Koogah suddenly tossed back his hoary head.

"Ho! Ho!" he laughed. "A foolish thing, this big canoe! A most foolish thing! The plaything of the wind! Wheresoever the wind goes, it goes too. No man who journeys therein may name the landing beach, for always he goes with the wind, and the wind goes everywhere, but no man knows where."

"It is so," Opee-Kwan supplemented gravely. "With the wind the going is easy, but against the wind a man striveth hard; and for that they had no paddles these men on the big canoe did not strive at all."

"Small need to strive," Nam-Bok cried angrily. "The schooner went likewise against the wind."

"And what said you made the sch—sch—schooner go?" Koogah asked, tripping craftily over the strange word.

"The wind," was the impatient response.

"Then the wind made the sch—sch—schooner go against the wind." Old Koogah dropped an open leer to Opee-Kwan, and, the laughter growing around him, continued: "The wind blows from the south and blows the schooner south. The wind blows against the wind. The wind blows one way and the other at the same time. It is very simple. We understand, Nam-Bok. We clearly understand."

"Thou art a fool!"

"Truth falls from thy lips," Koogah answered meekly. "I was over-long in understanding, and the thing was simple."

But Nam-Bok's face was dark, and he said rapid words which they had never heard before. Bone-scratching and skin-scraping were resumed, but he shut his lips tightly on the tongue that could not be believed.

"This sch—sch—schooner," Koogah imperturbably asked; "it was made of a big tree?"

"It was made of many trees," Nam-Bok snapped shortly. "It was very big."

He lapsed into sullen silence again, and Opee-Kwan nudged Koogah, who shook his head with slow amazement and murmured, "It is very strange."

Nam-Bok took the bait. "That is nothing," he said airily; "you should see the steamer. As the grain of sand is to the bidarka, as the bidarka is to the schooner, so the schooner is to the steamer. Further, the steamer is made of iron. It is all iron."

"Nay, nay, Nam-Bok," cried the head man; "how can that be? Always iron goes to the bottom. For behold, I received an iron knife in trade from the head man of the next village, and yesterday the iron knife slipped from my fingers and went down, down, into the sea. To all things there be law. Never was there one thing outside the law. This we know. And, moreover, we know that things of a kind have the one law, and that all iron has the one law. So unsay thy words, Nam-Bok, that we may yet honor thee."

"It is so," Nam-Bok persisted. "The steamer is all iron and does not sink."

"Nay, nay; this cannot be."

"With my own eyes I saw it."

"It is not in the nature of things."

"But tell me, Nam-Bok," Koogah interrupted, for fear the tale would go no farther, "tell me the manner of these men in finding their way across the sea when there is no land by which to steer."

"The sun points out the path."

"But how?"

"At midday the head man of the schooner takes a thing through which his eye looks at the sun, and then he makes the sun climb down out of the sky to the edge of the earth."

"Now this be evil medicine!" cried Opee-Kwan, aghast at the sacrilege. The men held up their hands in horror, and the women moaned. "This be evil medicine. It is not good to misdirect the great sun which drives away the night and gives us the seal, the salmon, and warm weather."

"What if it be evil medicine?" Nam-Bok demanded truculently. "I, too, have looked through the thing at the sun and made the sun climb down out of the sky."

Those who were nearest drew away from him hurriedly, and a woman covered the face of a child at her breast so that his eye might not fall upon it.

"But on the morning of the fourth day, O Nam-Bok," Koogah suggested; "on the morning of the fourth day when the sch—sch—schooner came after thee?"

"I had little strength left in me and could not run away. So I was taken on board and water was poured down my throat and good food given me. Twice, my brothers, you have seen a white man. These men were all white and as many as have I fingers and toes. And when I saw they were full of kindness, I took heart, and I resolved to bring away with me report of all that I saw. And they taught me the work they did, and gave me good food and a place to sleep.

"And day after day we went over the sea, and each day the head man drew the sun down out of the sky and made it tell where we were. And when the waves were kind, we hunted the fur seal and I marvelled much, for always did they fling the meat and the fat away and save only the skin."

Opee-Kwan's mouth was twitching violently, and he was about to make denunciation of such waste when Koogah kicked him to be still.

"After a weary time, when the sun was gone and the bite of the frost come into the air, the head man pointed the nose of the schooner south. South and east we traveled for days upon days, with never the land in sight, and we were near to the village from which hailed the men——"

"How did they know they were near?" Opee-Kwan, unable to contain himself longer, demanded. "There was no land to see."

Nam-Bok glowered on him wrathfully. "Did I not say the head man brought the sun down out of the sky?"

Koogah interposed, and Nam-Bok went on. "As I say, when we were near to that village a great storm blew up, and in the night we were helpless and knew not where we were——"

"Thou hast just said the head man knew——"

"Oh, peace, Opee-Kwan. Thou art a fool and cannot understand. As I say, we were helpless in the night, when I heard, above the roar of the storm, the sound of the sea on the beach. And next we struck with a mighty crash and I was in the water, swimming. It was a rock-bound coast, with one patch of beach in many miles, and the law was that I should dig my hands into the sand and draw myself clear of the surf. The other men must have pounded against the rocks, for none of them came ashore but the head man, and him I knew only by the ring on his finger.

"When day came, there being nothing of the schooner, I turned my face to the land and journeyed into it that I might get food and look upon the faces of the people. And when I came to a house I was taken in and given to eat, for I had learned their speech, and the white men are ever kindly. And it was a house bigger than all the houses built by us and our fathers before us."

"It was a mighty house," Koogah said, masking his unbelief with wonder.

"And many trees went into the making of such a house," Opee-Kwan added, taking the cue.

"That is nothing." Nam-Bok shrugged his shoulders in belittling fashion. "As our houses are to that house, so that house was to the houses I was yet to see."

"And they are not big men?"

"Nay; mere men like you and me," Nam-Bok answered. "I had cut a stick that I might walk in comfort, and remembering that I was to bring report to you, my brothers, I cut a notch in the stick for each person who lived in that house. And I stayed there many days, and worked, for which they gave me money—a thing of which you know nothing, but which is very good.

"And one day I departed from that place to go farther into the land. And as I walked I met many people, and I cut smaller notches in the stick, that there might be room for all. Then I came upon a strange thing. On the ground before me was a bar of iron, as big in thickness as my arm, and a long step away was another bar of iron"

"Then wert thou a rich man," Opee-Kwan asserted; "for iron be worth more than anything else in the world. It would have made many knives."

"Nay, it was not mine."

"It was a find, and a find be lawful."

"Not so; the white men had placed it there. And further, these bars were so long that no man could carry them away—so long that as far as I could see there was no end to them."

"Nam-Bok, that is very much iron," Opee-Kwan cautioned.

"Ay, it was hard to believe with my own eyes upon it; but I could not gainsay my eyes. And as I looked I heard ..." He turned abruptly upon the head man. "Opee-Kwan, thou hast heard the sea-lion bellow in his anger. Make it plain in thy mind of as many sea-lions as there be waves to the sea, and make it plain that all these sea-lions be made into one sea-lion, and as that one sea-lion would bellow so bellowed the thing I heard."

The fisherfolk cried aloud in astonishment, and Opee-Kwan's jaw lowered and remained lowered.

"And in the distance I saw a monster like unto a thousand whales. It was one-eyed, and vomited smoke, and it snorted with exceeding loudness. I was afraid and ran with shaking legs along the path between the bars. But it came with speed of the wind, this monster, and I leaped the iron bars with its breath hot on my face..."

Opee-Kwan gained control of his jaw again. "And—and then, O Nam-Bok?"

"Then it came by on the bars, and harmed me not; and when my legs could hold me up again it was gone from sight. And it is a very common thing in that country. Even the women and children are not afraid. Men make them to do work, these monsters."

"As we make our dogs do work?" Koogah asked, with sceptic twinkle in his eye.

"Ay, as we make our dogs do work."

"And how do they breed these—these things?" Opee-Kwan questioned.

"They breed not at all. Men fashion them cunningly of iron, and feed them with stone, and give them water to drink. The stone becomes fire, and the water becomes steam, and the steam of the water is the breath of their nostrils, and—"

"There, there, O Nam-Bok," Opee-Kwan interrupted. "Tell us of other wonders. We grow tired of this which we may not understand."

"You do not understand?" Nam-Bok asked despairingly.

"Nay, we do not understand," the men and women wailed back. "We cannot understand."

Nam-Bok thought of a combined harvester, and of the machines wherein visions of living men were to be seen, and of the machines from which came the voices of men, and he knew his people could never understand.

"Dare I say I rode this iron monster through the land?" he asked bitterly.

Opee-Kwan threw up his hands, palms outward, in open incredulity. "Say on; say anything. We listen."

"Then did I ride the iron monster, for which I gave money—"

"Thou saidst it was fed with stone."

"And likewise, thou fool, I said money was a thing of which

you know nothing. As I say, I rode the monster through the land, and through many villages, until I came to a big village on a salt arm of the sea. And the houses shoved their roofs among the stars in the sky, and the clouds drifted by them, and everywhere was much smoke. And the roar of that village was like the roar of the sea in storm, and the people were so many that I flung away my stick and no longer remembered the notches upon it."

"Hadst thou made small notches," Koogah reproved, "thou mightst have brought report."

Nam-Bok whirled upon him in anger. "Had I made small notches! Listen, Koogah, thou scratcher of bone! If I had made small notches neither the stick, nor twenty sticks, could have borne them—nay, not all the driftwood of all the beaches between this village and the next. And if all of you, the women and children as well, were twenty times as many, and if you had twenty hands each, and in each hand a stick and a knife, still the notches could not be cut for the people I saw, so many were they and so fast did they come and go."

"There cannot be so many people in all the world," Opee-Kwan objected, for he was stunned and his mind could not grasp such magnitude of numbers.

"What dost thou know of all the world and how large it is?" Nam-Bok demanded.

"But there cannot be so many people in one place."

"Who art thou to say what can be and what cannot be?"

"It stands to reason there cannot be so many people in one place. Their canoes would clutter the sea till there was no room. And they could empty the sea each day of its fish, and they would not all be fed."

"So it would seem," Nam-Bok made final answer; "yet it was so. With my own eyes I saw, and flung my stick away." He yawned heavily and rose to his feet. "I have paddled far. The day has been long, and I am tired. Now I will sleep, and to-morrow we will have further talk upon the things I have seen."

Bask-Wah-Wan, hobbling fearfully in advance, proud indeed, yet awed by her wonderful son, led him to her igloo and stowed him away among the greasy, ill-smelling furs. But the men lingered by the fire, and a council was held wherein was there much whispering and low-voiced discussion.

An hour passed, and a second, and Nam-Bok slept, and the talk went on. The evening sun dipped toward the northwest, and at eleven at night was nearly due north. Then it was that the head man and the bone-scratcher separated themselves from the council and aroused Nam-Bok. He blinked up into their faces and turned on his side to sleep again. Opee-Kwan gripped him by the arm and kindly but firmly shook his senses back into him.

"Come, Nam-Bok, arise!" he commanded. "It be time."

"Another feast!" Nam-Bok cried. "Nay, I am not hungry. Go on with the eating and let me sleep."

"Time to be gone!" Koogah thundered.

But Opee-Kwan spoke more softly. "Thou wast bidarka-mate with me when we were boys," he said. "Together we first chased the seal and drew the salmon from the traps. And thou didst drag me back to life, Nam-Bok, when the sea closed over me and I was sucked down to the black rocks. Together we hungered and bore the chill of the frost, and together we crawled beneath the one fur and lay close to each other. And because of these things, and the kindness in which I stood to thee, it grieves me sore that thou shouldst return such a remarkable liar. We cannot understand, and our heads be dizzy with the things thou hast spoken. It is not good, and there has been much talk in the council. Wherefore we send thee away, that our heads may remain clear and strong and be not troubled by the unaccountable things."

"These things thou speakest of be shadows," Koogah took up the strain. "From the shadow-world thou hast brought them, and to the shadow-world thou must return them. Thy bidarka be ready, and the tribespeople wait. They may not sleep until thou art gone."

Nam-Bok was perplexed, but hearkened to the voice of the head man.

"If thou art Nam-Bok," Opee-Kwan was saying, "thou art a fearful and most wonderful liar; if thou art the shadow of Nam-Bok, then thou speakest of shadows, concerning which it is not good that living men have knowledge. This great village thou hast spoken of we deem the village of shadows. Therein flutter the souls of the dead; for the dead be many and the living few. The dead do not come back. Never have the dead come back—save thou with thy wonder-tales. It is not meet that the dead come back, and should we permit it, great trouble may be our portion."

Nam-Bok knew his people well and was aware that the voice of the council was supreme. So he allowed himself to be led down to the water's edge, where he was put aboard his bidarka and a paddle thrust into his hand. A stray wildfowl honked somewhere to seaward, and the surf broke limply and hollowly on the sand. A dim twilight brooded over land and water, and in the north the sun smouldered, vague and troubled, and draped about with blood-red mists. The gulls were flying low. The off-shore wind blew keen and chill, and the black-massed clouds behind it gave promise of bitter weather.

"Out of the sea thou earnest," Opee-Kwan chanted oracularly, "and back into the sea thou goest. Thus is balance achieved and all things brought to law."

Bask-Wah-Wan limped to the froth-mark and cried, "I bless thee, Nam-Bok, for that thou remembered me."

But Koogah, shoving Nam-Bok clear or the beach, tore the shawl from her shoulders and flung it into the bidarka.

"It is cold in the long nights," she wailed; "and the frost is prone to nip old bones."

"The thing is a shadow," the bone-scratcher answered, "and shadows cannot keep thee warm."

Nam-Bok stood up that his voice might carry. "O Bask-Wah-Wan, mother that bore me!" he called. "Listen to the words of Nam-Bok, thy son. There be room in his bidarka for two, and he would that thou earnest with him. For his journey is to where there are fish and oil in plenty. There the frost comes not, and life is easy, and the things of iron do the work of men. Wilt thou come, O Bask-Wah-Wan?"

She debated a moment, while the bidarka drifted swiftly from her, then raised her voice to a quavering treble. "I am old, Nam-Bok, and soon I shall pass down among the shadows. But I have no wish to go before my time. I am old, Nam-Bok, and I am afraid."

A shaft of light shot across the dim-lit sea and wrapped boat and man in a splendor of red and gold. Then a hush fell upon the fisherfolk, and only was heard the moan of the off-shore wind and the cries of the gulls flying low in the air.

YELLOW HANDKERCHIEF

"I'm not wanting to dictate to you, lad," Charley said, "but I'm very much against your making a last raid. You've gone safely through rough times with rough men, and it would be a shame to have something happen to you at the very end."

"But how can I get out of making a last raid?" I demanded, with the cocksureness of youth. "There always has to be a last, you know, to anything."

Charley crossed his legs, leaned back, and considered the problem. "Very true. But why not call the capture of Demetrios Contos the last? You're back from it safe and sound and hearty, for all your good wetting, and—and——" His voice broke and he could not speak for a moment. "And I could never forgive myself if anything happened to you now."

I laughed at Charley's fears while I gave in to the claims of his affection, and agreed to consider the last raid already performed. We had been together for two years, and now I was leaving the fish patrol in order to go back and finish my education. I had earned and saved money to put me through three years at the high school, and though the beginning of the term was several months away, I intended doing a lot of studying for the entrance examinations.

My belongings were packed snugly in a sea-chest, and I was all ready to buy my ticket and ride down on the train to Oakland, when Neil Partington arrived in Benicia. The Reindeer was needed immediately for work far down on the Lower Bay, and Neil said he intended to run straight for Oakland. As that was his home and as I was to live with his family while going to school, he saw no reason, he said, why I should not put my chest aboard and come along.

So the chest went aboard, and in the middle of the afternoon we hoisted the Reindeer's big mainsail and cast off. It was tantalizing fall weather. The sea-breeze, which had blown steadily all summer, was gone, and in its place were capricious winds and murky skies which made the time of arriving anywhere extremely problematical. We started on the first of the ebb, and as we slipped down the Carquinez Straits, I looked my last for some time upon Benicia and the bight at Turner's Shipyard, where we had besieged the Lancashire Queen, and had captured Big Alec, the King of the Greeks. And at the mouth of the Straits I looked with not a little interest upon the spot where a few days before I should have drowned but for the good that was in the nature of Demetrios Contos.

A great wall of fog advanced across San Pablo Bay to meet us, and in a few minutes the Reindeer was running blindly through the damp obscurity. Charley, who was steering, seemed to have an instinct for that kind of work. How he did it, he himself confessed that he did not know; but he had a way of calculating winds, currents, distance, time, drift, and sailing speed that was truly marvellous.

"It looks as though it were lifting," Neil Partington said, a couple of hours after we had entered the fog. "Where do you say we are, Charley?"

Charley looked at his watch. "Six o'clock, and three hours more of ebb," he remarked casually.

"But where do you say we are!" Neil insisted.

Charley pondered a moment, and then answered, "The tide has edged us over a bit out of our course, but if the fog lifts right now, as it is going to lift, you'll find we're not more than a thousand miles off McNear's Landing."

"You might be a little more definite by a few miles, anyway," Neil grumbled, showing by his tone that he disagreed.

"All right, then," Charley said, conclusively, "not less than a quarter of a mile, nor more than a half."

The wind freshened with a couple of little puffs, and the fog thinned perceptibly.

"McNear's is right off there," Charley said, pointing directly into the fog on our weather beam.

The three of us were peering intently in that direction, when the Reindeer struck with a dull crash and came to a standstill. We ran forward, and found her bowsprit entangled in the tanned rigging of a short, chunky mast. She had collided, head on, with a Chinese junk lying at anchor.

At the moment we arrived forward, five Chinese, like so many bees, came swarming out of the little 'tween-decks cabin, the sleep still in their eyes.

Leading them came a big, muscular man, conspicuous for his pock-marked face and the yellow silk handkerchief swathed about his head. It was Yellow Handkerchief, the Chinaman whom we had arrested for illegal shrimp-fishing the year before, and who, at that time, had nearly sunk the Reindeer, as he had nearly sunk it now by violating the rules of navigation.

"What d'ye mean, you yellow-faced heathen, lying here in a fairway without a horn a-going?" Charley cried hotly.

"Mean?" Neil calmly answered. "Just take a look—that's what he means."

Our eyes followed the direction indicated by Neil's finger, and we saw the open amidships of the junk, half filled, as we found on closer examination, with fresh-caught shrimps. Mingled with the shrimps were myriads of small fish, from a quarter of an inch upward in size. Yellow Handkerchief had lifted the trap-net at high-water slack, and, taking advantage of the concealment offered by the fog, had boldly been lying by, waiting to lift the net again at low-water slack.

"Well," Neil hummed and hawed, "in all my varied and extensive experience as a fish patrolman, I must say this is the easiest capture I ever made. What'll we do with them, Charley?"

"Tow the junk into San Rafael, of course," came the answer. Charley turned to me. "You stand by the junk, lad, and I'll pass you a towing line. If the wind doesn't fail us, we'll make the creek before the tide gets too low, sleep at San Rafael, and arrive in Oakland to-morrow by midday."

So saying, Charley and Neil returned to the Reindeer and got under way, the junk towing astern. I went aft and took charge of the prize, steering by means of an antiquated tiller and a rudder with large, diamond-shaped holes, through which the water rushed back and forth.

By now the last of the fog had vanished, and Charley's estimate of our position was confirmed by the sight of McNear's Landing a short half-mile away, following: along the west shore, we rounded Point Pedro in plain view of the Chinese shrimp villages, and a great to-do was raised when they saw one of their junks towing behind the familiar fish patrol sloop.

The wind, coming off the land, was rather puffy and uncertain, and it would have been more to our advantage had it been stronger. San Rafael Creek, up which we had to go to reach the town and turn over our prisoners to the authorities, ran through wide-stretching marshes, and was difficult to navigate on a falling tide, while at low tide it was impossible to navigate at all. So, with the tide already half-ebbed, it was necessary for us to make time. This the heavy junk prevented, lumbering along behind and holding the Reindeer back by just so much dead weight.

"Tell those coolies to get up that sail," Charley finally called to me. "We don't want to hang up on the mud flats for the rest of the night."

I repeated the order to Yellow Handkerchief, who mumbled it huskily to his men. He was suffering from a bad cold, which doubled him up in convulsive coughing spells and made his eyes heavy and bloodshot. This made him more evil-looking than ever, and when he glared viciously at me I remembered with a shiver the close shave I had had with him at the time of his previous arrest.

His crew sullenly tailed on to the halyards, and the strange, outlandish sail, lateen in rig and dyed a warm brown, rose in the air. We were sailing on the wind, and when Yellow Handkerchief flattened down the sheet the junk forged ahead and the tow-line went slack. Fast as the Reindeer could sail, the junk outsailed her; and to avoid running her down I hauled a little closer on the wind. But the junk likewise outpointed, and in a couple of minutes I was abreast of the Reindeer and to windward. The tow-line had now tautened, at right angles to the two boats, and the predicament was laughable.

"Cast off!" I shouted.

Charley hesitated.

"It's all right," I added. "Nothing can happen. We'll make the creek on this tack, and you'll be right behind me all the way up to San Rafael."

At this Charley cast off, and Yellow Handkerchief sent one of his men forward to haul in the line. In the gathering darkness I could just make out the mouth of San Rafael Creek, and by the time we entered it I could barely see its banks. The Reindeer was fully five minutes astern, and we continued to leave her astern as we beat up the narrow, winding channel. With Charley behind us, it seemed I had little to fear from my five prisoners; but the darkness prevented my keeping a sharp eye on them, so I transferred my revolver from my trousers pocket to the side pocket of my coat, where I could more quickly put my hand on it.

Yellow Handkerchief was the one I feared, and that he knew it and made use of it, subsequent events will show. He was sitting a few feet away from me, on what then happened to be the weather side of the junk. I could scarcely see the outlines of his form, but I soon became convinced that he was slowly, very slowly, edging closer to me. I watched him carefully. Steering with my left hand, I slipped my right into my pocket and got hold of the revolver.

I saw him shift along for a couple of inches, and I was just about to order him back—the words were trembling on the tip of my tongue—when I was struck with great force by a heavy figure that had leaped through the air upon me from the lee side. It was one of the crew. He pinioned my right arm so that I could not withdraw my hand from my pocket, and at the same time clapped his other hand over my mouth. Of course, I could have struggled away from him and freed my hand or gotten my mouth clear so that I might cry an alarm, but in a trice Yellow Handkerchief was on top of me.

I struggled around to no purpose in the bottom of the junk, while my legs and arms were tied and my mouth securely bound in what I afterward found to be a cotton shirt. Then I was left lying in the bottom. Yellow Handkerchief took the tiller, issuing his orders in whispers; and from our position at the time, and from the alteration of the sail, which I could dimly make out above me as a blot against the stars, I knew the junk was being headed into the mouth of a small slough which emptied at that point into San Rafael Creek.

In a couple of minutes we ran softly alongside the bank, and the sail was silently lowered. The Chinese kept very quiet. Yellow Handkerchief sat down in the bottom alongside of me, and I could feel him straining to repress his raspy, hacking cough. Possibly seven or eight minutes later I heard Charley's voice as the Reindeer went past the mouth of the slough.

"I can't tell you how relieved I am," I could plainly hear him saying to Neil, "that the lad has finished with the fish patrol without accident."

Here Neil said something which I could not catch, and then Charley's voice went on:

"The youngster takes naturally to the water, and if when he finishes high school he takes a course in navigation and goes deep sea, I see no reason why he shouldn't rise to be master of the finest and biggest ship afloat."

It was all very flattering to me, but lying there, bound and gagged by my own prisoners, with the voices growing faint and fainter as the Reindeer slipped on through the darkness toward San Rafael, I must say I was not in quite the proper situation to enjoy my smiling future. With the Reindeer went my last hope. What was to happen next I could not imagine, for the Chinese were a different race from mine and from what I knew I was confident that fair play was no part of their make-up.

After waiting a few minutes longer, the crew hoisted the lateen sail, and Yellow Handkerchief steered down toward the mouth of San Rafael Creek. The tide was getting lower, and he had difficulty in escaping the mud-banks. I was hoping he would run aground, but he succeeded in making the bay without accident.

As we passed out of the creek a noisy discussion arose, which I knew related to me. Yellow Handkerchief was vehement, but the other four as vehemently opposed him. It was very evident that he advocated doing away with me and that they were afraid of the consequences. I was familiar enough with the Chinese character to know that fear alone restrained them. But what plan they offered in place of Yellow Handkerchief's murderous one, I could not make out.

My feelings, as my fate hung in the balance, may be guessed. The discussion developed into a quarrel, in the midst of which Yellow Handkerchief unshipped the heavy tiller and sprang toward me. But his four companions threw themselves between, and a clumsy struggle took place for possession of the tiller. In the end Yellow Handkerchief was overcome, and sullenly returned to the steering, while they soundly berated him for his rashness.

Not long after, the sail was run down and the junk slowly urged forward by means of the sweeps. I felt it ground gently on the soft mud. Three of the Chinese—they all wore long sea-boots—got over the side, and the other two passed me across the rail. With Yellow Handkerchief at my legs and his two companions at my shoulders, they began to flounder along through the mud. After some time their feet struck firmer footing, and I knew they were carrying me up some beach. The location of this beach was not doubtful in my mind. It could be none other than one of the Marin Islands, a group of rocky islets which lay off the Marin County shore.

When they reached the firm sand that marked high tide, I was dropped, and none too gently. Yellow Handkerchief kicked me spitefully in the ribs, and then the trio floundered back through the mud to the junk. A moment later I heard the sail go up and slat in the wind as they drew in the sheet. Then silence fell, and I was left to my own devices for getting free.

I remembered having seen tricksters writhe and squirm out of ropes with which they were bound, but though I writhed and squirmed like a good fellow, the knots remained as hard as ever, and there was no appreciable slack. In the course of my squirming, however, I rolled over upon a heap of clam-shells—the remains, evidently, of some yachting party's clam-bake. This gave me an idea. My hands were tied behind my back; and, clutching a shell in them, I rolled over and over, up the beach, till I came to the rocks I knew to be there.

Rolling around and searching, I finally discovered a narrow crevice, into which I shoved the shell. The edge of it was sharp, and across the sharp edge I proceeded to saw the rope that bound my wrists. The edge of the shell was also brittle, and I broke it by bearing too heavily upon it. Then I rolled back to the heap and returned with as many shells as I could carry in both hands. I broke many shells, cut my hands a number of times, and got cramps in my legs from my strained position and my exertions.

While I was suffering from the cramps, and resting, I heard a familiar halloo drift across the water. It was Charley, searching for me. The gag in my mouth prevented me from replying, and I could only lie there, helplessly fuming, while he rowed past the island and his voice slowly lost itself in the distance.

I returned to the sawing process, and at the end of half an hour succeeded in severing the rope. The rest was easy. My hands once free, it was a matter of minutes to loosen my legs and to take the gag out of my mouth. I ran around the island to make sure it was an island and not by any chance a portion of the mainland. An island it certainly was, one of the Marin group, fringed with a sandy beach and surrounded by a sea of mud. Nothing remained but to wait till daylight and to keep warm; for it was a cold, raw night for California, with just enough wind to pierce the skin and cause one to shiver.

To keep up the circulation, I ran around the island a dozen times or so, and clambered across its rocky backbone as many times more—all of which was of greater service to me, as I afterward discovered, than merely to warm me up. In the midst of this exercise I wondered if I had lost anything out of my pockets while rolling over and over in the sand. A search showed the absence of my revolver and pocket-knife. The first Yellow Handkerchief had taken; but the knife had been lost in the sand.

I was hunting for it when the sound of rowlocks came to my ears. At first, of course, I thought of Charley; but on second thought I knew Charley would be calling out as he rowed along. A sudden premonition of danger seized me. The Marin Islands are lonely places; chance visitors in the dead of night are hardly to be expected. What if it were Yellow Handkerchief? The sound made by the rowlocks grew more distinct. I crouched in the sand and listened intently. The boat, which I judged a small skiff from the quick stroke of the oars, was landing in the mud about fifty yards up the beach. I heard a raspy, hacking cough, and my heart stood still. It was Yellow Handkerchief. Not to be robbed of his revenge by his more cautious companions, he had stolen away from the village and come back alone.

I did some swift thinking. I was unarmed and helpless on a tiny islet, and a yellow barbarian, whom I had reason to fear, was coming after me. Any place was safer than the island, and I turned instinctively to the water, or rather to the mud. As he began to flounder ashore through the mud, I started to flounder out into it, going over the same course which the Chinese had taken in landing me and in returning to the junk.

Yellow Handkerchief, believing me to be lying tightly bound, exercised no care, but came ashore noisily. This helped me, for, under the shield of his noise and making no more myself than necessary, I managed to cover fifty feet by the time he had made the beach. Here I lay down in the mud. It was cold and clammy, and made me shiver, but I did not care to stand up and run the risk of being discovered by his sharp eyes.

He walked down the beach straight to where he had left me lying, and I had a fleeting feeling of regret at not being able to see his surprise when he did not find me. But it was a very fleeting regret, for my teeth were chattering with the cold.

What his movements were after that I had largely to deduce from the facts of the situation, for I could scarcely see him in the dim starlight. But I was sure that the first thing he did was to make the circuit of the beach to learn if landings had been made by other boats. This he would have known at once by the tracks through the mud.

Convinced that no boat had removed me from the island, he next started to find out what had become of me. Beginning at the pile of clam-shells, he lighted matches to trace my tracks in the sand. At such times I could see his villainous face plainly, and, when the sulphur from the matches irritated his lungs, between the raspy cough that followed and the clammy mud in which I was lying, I confess I shivered harder than ever.

The multiplicity of my footprints puzzled him. Then the idea that I might be out in the mud must have struck him, for he waded out a few yards in my direction, and, stooping, with his eyes searched the dim surface long and carefully. He could not have been more than fifteen feet from me, and had he lighted a match he would surely have discovered me.

He returned to the beach and clambered about over the rocky backbone, again hunting for me with lighted matches. The closeness of the shave impelled me to further flight. Not daring to wade upright, on account of the noise made by floundering and by the suck of the mud, I remained lying down in the mud and propelled myself over its surface by means of my hands. Still keeping the trail made by the Chinese in going from and to the junk, I held on until I reached the water. Into this I waded to a depth of three feet, and then I turned off to the side on a line parallel with the beach.

The thought came to me of going toward Yellow Handkerchief's skiff and escaping in it, but at that very moment he returned to the beach, and, as though fearing the very thing I had in mind, he slushed out through the mud to assure himself that the skiff was safe. This turned me in the opposite direction. Half swimming, half wading, with my head just out of water and avoiding splashing, I succeeded in putting about a hundred feet between myself and the spot where the Chinese had begun to wade ashore from the junk. I drew myself out on the mud and remained lying flat.

Again Yellow Handkerchief returned to the beach and made a search of the island, and again he returned to the heap of clam-shells. I knew what was running in his mind as well as he did himself. No one could leave or land without making tracks in the mud. The only tracks to be seen were those leading from his skiff and from where the junk had been. I was not on the island. I must have left it by one or the other of those two tracks. He had just been over the one to his skiff, and was certain I had not left that way. Therefore I could have left the island only by going over the tracks of the junk landing. This he proceeded to verify by wading out over them himself, lighting matches as he came along.

When he arrived at the point where I had first lain, I knew, by the matches he burned and the time he took, that he had discovered the marks left by my body. These he followed straight to the water and into it, but in three feet of water he could no longer see them. On the other hand, as the tide was still falling, he could easily make out the impression made by the junk's bow, and could have likewise made out the impression of any other boat if it had landed at that particular spot. But there was no such mark; and I knew that he was absolutely convinced that I was hiding somewhere in the mud.

But to hunt on a dark night for a boy in a sea of mud would be like hunting for a needle in a haystack, and he did not attempt it. Instead he went back to the beach and prowled around for some time. I was hoping he would give me up and go, for by this time I was suffering severely from the cold. At last he waded out to his skiff and rowed away. What if this departure of Yellow Handkerchief's were a sham? What if he had done it merely to entice me ashore?

The more I thought of it the more certain I became that he had made a little too much noise with his oars as he rowed away. So I remained, lying in the mud and shivering. I shivered till the muscles of the small of my back ached and pained me as badly as the cold, and I had need of all my self-control to force myself to remain in my miserable situation.

It was well that I did, however, for, possibly an hour later, I thought I could make out something moving on the beach. I watched intently, but my ears were rewarded first, by a raspy cough I knew only too well. Yellow Handkerchief had sneaked back, landed on the other side of the island, and crept around to surprise me if I had returned.

After that, though hours passed without sign of him, I was afraid to return to the island at all. On the other hand, I was almost equally afraid that I should die of the exposure I was undergoing. I had never dreamed one could suffer so. I grew so cold and numb, finally, that I ceased to shiver. But my muscles and bones began to ache in a way that was agony. The tide had long since begun to rise and, foot by foot, it drove me in toward the beach. High water came at three o'clock, and at three o'clock I drew myself up on the beach, more dead than alive, and too helpless to have offered any resistance had Yellow Handkerchief swooped down upon me.

But no Yellow Handkerchief appeared. He had given me up and gone back to Point Pedro. Nevertheless, I was in a deplorable, not to say a dangerous, condition. I could not stand upon my feet, much less walk. My clammy, muddy garments clung to me like sheets of ice. I thought I should never get them off. So numb and lifeless were my fingers, and so weak was I that it seemed to take an hour to get off my shoes. I had not the strength to break the porpoise-hide laces, and the knots defied me. I repeatedly beat my hands upon the rocks to get some sort of life into them. Sometimes I felt sure I was going to die.

But in the end,—after several centuries, it seemed to me,—I got off the last of my clothes. The water was now close at hand, and I crawled painfully into it and washed the mud from my naked body. Still, I could not get on my feet and walk and I was afraid to lie still. Nothing remained but to crawl weakly, like a snail, and at the cost of constant pain, up and down the sand. I kept this up as long as possible, but as the east paled with the coming of dawn I began to succumb. The sky grew rosy-red, and the golden rim of the sun, showing above the horizon, found me lying helpless and motionless among the clam-shells.

As in a dream, I saw the familiar mainsail of the Reindeer as she slipped out of San Rafael Creek on a light puff of morning air. This dream was very much broken. There are intervals I can never recollect on looking back over it. Three things, however, I distinctly remember: the first sight of the Reindeer's mainsail; her lying at anchor a few hundred feet away and a small boat leaving her side; and the cabin stove roaring red-hot, myself swathed all over with blankets, except on the chest and shoulders, which Charley was pounding and mauling unmercifully, and my mouth and throat burning with the coffee which Neil Partington was pouring down a trifle too hot.

But burn or no burn, I tell you it felt good. By the time we arrived in Oakland I was as limber and strong as ever,—though Charley and Neil Partington were afraid I was going to have pneumonia, and Mrs. Partington, for my first six months of school, kept an anxious eye upon me to discover the first symptoms of consumption.

Time flies. It seems but yesterday that I was a lad of sixteen on the fish patrol. Yet I know that I arrived this very morning from China, with a quick passage to my credit, and master of the barkentine Harvester. And I know that to-morrow morning I shall run over to Oakland to see Neil Partington and his wife and family, and later on up to Benicia to see Charley Le Grant and talk over old times. No; I shall not go to Benicia, now that I think about it. I expect to be a highly interested party to a wedding, shortly to take place. Her name is Alice Partington, and, since Charley has promised to be best man, he will have to come down to Oakland instead.

MAKE WESTING

Whatever you do, make westing! make westing! —Sailing directions for Cape Horn.

For seven weeks the Mary Rogers had been between 50° south in the Atlantic and 50° south in the Pacific, which meant that for seven weeks she had been struggling to round Cape Horn. For seven weeks she had been either in dirt, or close to dirt, save once, and then, following upon six days of excessive dirt, which she had ridden out under the shelter of the redoubtable Terra Del Fuego coast, she had almost gone ashore during a heavy swell in the dead calm that had suddenly fallen. For seven weeks she had wrestled with the Cape Horn gray-beards, and in return been buffeted and smashed by them. She was a wooden ship, and her ceaseless straining had opened her seams, so that twice a day the watch took its turn at the pumps.

The Mary Rogers was strained, the crew was strained, and big Dan Cullen, master, was likewise strained. Perhaps he was strained most of all, for upon him rested the responsibility of that titanic struggle. He slept most of the time in his clothes, though he rarely slept. He haunted the deck at night, a great, burly, robust ghost, black with the sunburn of thirty years of sea and hairy as an orang-utan. He, in turn, was haunted by one thought of action, a sailing direction for the Horn: Whatever you do, make westing! make westing! It was an obsession. He thought of nothing else, except, at times, to blaspheme God for sending such bitter weather.

Make westing! He hugged the Horn, and a dozen times lay hove to with the iron Cape bearing east-by-north, or north-north-east, a score of miles away. And each time the eternal west wind smote him back and he made easting. He fought gale after gale, south to 64°, inside the antarctic drift-ice, and pledged his immortal soul to the Powers of Darkness for a bit of westing, for a slant to take him around. And he made easting. In despair, he had tried to make the passage through the Straits of Le Maire. Halfway through, the wind hauled to the north 'ard of northwest, the glass dropped to 28.88, and he turned and ran before a gale of cyclonic fury, missing, by a hair's breadth, piling up the Mary Rogers on the black-toothed rocks. Twice he had made west to the Diego Ramirez Rocks, one of the times saved between two snow-squalls by sighting the gravestones of ships a quarter of a mile dead ahead.

Blow! Captain Dan Cullen instanced all his thirty years at sea to prove that never had it blown so before. The Mary Rogers was hove to at the time he gave the evidence, and, to clinch it, inside half an hour the Mary Rogers was hove down to the hatches. Her new main-topsail and brand new spencer were blown away like tissue paper; and five sails, furled and fast under double gaskets, were blown loose and stripped from the yards. And before morning the Mary Rogers was hove down twice again, and holes were knocked in her bulwarks to ease her decks from the weight of ocean that pressed her down.

On an average of once a week Captain Dan Cullen caught glimpses of the sun. Once, for ten minutes, the sun shone at midday, and ten minutes afterward a new gale was piping up, both watches were shortening sail, and all was buried in the obscurity of a driving snow-squall. For a fortnight, once, Captain Dan Cullen was without a meridian or a chronometer sight. Rarely did he know his position within half a degree, except when in sight of land; for sun and stars remained hidden behind the sky, and it was so gloomy that even at the best the horizons were poor for accurate observations. A gray gloom shrouded the world. The clouds were gray; the great driving seas were leaden gray gloom shrouded the world. The clouds were gray; the great driving seas were leadening; even the occasional albatrosses were gray, while the snow-flurries were not white, but gray, under the sombre pall of the heavens.

Life on board the Mary Rogers was gray,—gray and gloomy. The faces of the sailors were blue-gray; they were afflicted with sea-cuts and sea-boils, and suffered exquisitely. They were shadows of men. For seven weeks, in the forecastle or on deck, they had not known what it was to be dry. They had forgotten what it was to sleep out a watch, and all watches it was, "All hands on deck!" They caught snatches of agonized sleep, and they slept in their oilskins ready for the everlasting call. So weak and worn were they that it took both watches to do the work of one. That was why both watches were on deck so much of the time. And no shadow of a man could shirk duty. Nothing less than a broken leg could enable a man to knock off work; and there were two such, who had been mauled and pulped by the seas that broke aboard.

One other man who was the shadow of a man was George Dorety. He was the only passenger on board, a friend of the firm, and he had elected to make the voyage for his health. But seven weeks of Cape Horn had not bettered his health. He gasped and panted in his bunk through the long, heaving nights; and when on deck he was so bundled up for warmth that he resembled a peripatetic old-clothes shop. At midday, eating at the cabin table in a gloom so deep that the swinging sea-lamps burned always, he looked as blue-gray as the sickest, saddest man for'ard. Nor did gazing across the table at Captain Dan Cullen have any cheering effect upon him. Captain Cullen chewed and scowled and kept silent. The scowls were for God, and with every chew he reiterated the sole thought of his existence, which was make westing. He was a big, hairy brute, and the sight of him was not stimulating to the other's appetite. He looked upon George Dorety as a Jonah, and told him so, once each meal, savagely transferring the scowl from God to the passenger and back again.

Nor did the mate prove a first aid to a languid appetite. Joshua Higgins by name, a seaman by profession and pull, but a pot-wolloper by capacity, he was a loose-jointed, sniffling creature, heartless and selfish and cowardly, without a soul, in fear of his life of Dan Cullen, and a bully over the sailors, who knew that behind the mate was Captain Cullen, the lawgiver and compeller, the driver and the destroyer, the incarnation of a dozen bucko mates. In that wild weather at the southern end of the earth, Joshua Higgins ceased washing. His grimy face usually robbed George Dorety of what little appetite he managed to accumulate. Ordinarily this lavatorial dereliction would have caught Captain Cullen's eye and vocabulary, but in the present his mind was filled with making westing, to the exclusion of all other things not contributory thereto. Whether the mate's face was clean or dirty had no bearing upon westing. Later on, when 50° south in the Pacific had been reached, Joshua Higgins would wash his face very abruptly. In the meantime, at the cabin table, where gray twilight alternated with lamplight while the lamps were being filled, George Dorety sat between the two men, one a tiger and the other a hyena, and wondered why God had made them. The second mate, Matthew Turner, was a true sailor and a man, but George Dorety did not have the solace of his company, for he ate by himself, solitary, when they had finished.

On Saturday morning, July 24, George Dorety awoke to a feeling of life and headlong movement. On deck he found the Mary Rogers running off before a howling southeaster. Nothing was set but the lower topsails and the foresail. It was all she could stand, yet she was making fourteen knots, as Mr. Turner shouted in Dorety's ear when he came on deck. And it was all westing. She was going around the Horn at last ... if the wind held. Mr. Turner looked happy. The end of the struggle was in sight. But Captain Cullen did not look happy. He scowled at Dorety in passing. Captain Cullen did not want God to know that he was pleased with that wind. He had a conception of a malicious God, and believed in his secret soul that if God knew it was a desirable wind, God would promptly efface it and send a snorter from the west. So he walked softly before God, smothering his joy down under scowls and muttered curses, and, so, fooling God, for God was the only thing in the universe of which Dan Cullen was afraid.

All Saturday and Saturday night the Mary Rogers raced her westing. Persistently she logged her fourteen knots, so that by Sunday morning she had covered three hundred and fifty miles. If the wind held, she would make around. If it failed, and the snorter came from anywhere between southwest and north, back the Mary Rogers would be hurled and be no better off than she had been seven weeks before. And on Sunday morning the wind was failing. The big sea was going down and running smooth. Both watches were on deck setting sail after sail as fast as the ship could stand it. And now Captain Cullen went around brazenly before God, smoking a big cigar, smiling jubilantly, as if the failing wind delighted him, while down underneath he was raging against God for taking the life out of the blessed wind. Make westing! So he would, if God would only leave him alone. Secretly, he pledged himself anew to the Powers of Darkness, if they would let him make westing. He pledged himself so easily because he did not believe in the Powers of Darkness. He really believed only in God, though he did not know it. And in his inverted theology God was really the Prince of Darkness. Captain Cullen was a devil-worshipper, but he called the devil by another name, that was all.

At midday, after calling eight bells, Captain Cullen ordered the royals on. The men went aloft faster than they had gone in weeks. Not alone were they nimble because of the westing, but a benignant sun was shining down and limbering their stiff bodies. George Dorety stood aft, near Captain Cullen, less bundled in clothes than usual, soaking in the grateful warmth as he watched the scene. Swiftly and abruptly the incident occurred. There was a cry from the foreroyal-yard of "Man overboard!" Somebody threw a life buoy over the side, and at the same instant the second mate's voice came aft, ringing and peremptory:—

"Hard down your helm!"

The man at the wheel never moved a spoke. He knew better, for Captain Dan Cullen was standing alongside of him. He wanted to move a spoke, to move all the spokes, to grind the wheel down, hard down, for his comrade drowning in the sea. He glanced at Captain Dan Cullen, and Captain Dan Cullen gave no sign.

"Down! Hard down!" the second mate roared, as he sprang aft.

But he ceased springing and commanding, and stood still, when he saw Dan Cullen by the wheel. And big Dan Cullen puffed at his cigar and said nothing. Astern, and going astern fast, could be seen the sailor. He had caught the life buoy and was clinging to it. Nobody spoke. Nobody moved. The men aloft clung to the royal yards and watched with terror stricken faces. And the Mary Rogers raced on, making her westing. A long, silent minute passed.

"Who was it!" Captain Cullen demanded.

"Mops, sir," eagerly answered the sailor at the wheel.

Mops topped a wave astern and disappeared temporarily in the trough. It was a large wave, but it was no graybeard. A small boat could live easily in such a sea, and in such a sea the Mary Rogers could easily come to. But she could not come to and make westing at the same time.

For the first time in all his years, George Dorety was seeing a real drama of life and death—a sordid little drama in which the scales balanced an unknown sailor named Mops against a few miles of longitude. At first he had watched the man astern, but now he watched big Dan Cullen, hairy and black, vested with power of life and death, smoking a cigar.

Captain Dan Cullen smoked another long, silent minute. Then he removed the cigar from his mouth. He glanced aloft at the spars of the Mary Rogers, and overside at the sea.

"Sheet home the royals!" he cried.

Fifteen minutes later they sat at table, in the cabin, with food served before them. On one side of George Dorety sat Dan Cullen, the tiger, on the other side, Joshua Higgins, the hyena. Nobody spoke. On deck the men were sheeting home the skysails. George Dorety could hear their cries, while a persistent vision haunted him of a man called Mops, alive and well, clinging to a life buoy miles astern in that lonely ocean. He glanced at Captain Cullen, and experienced a feeling of nausea, for the man was eating his food with relish, almost bolting it.

"Captain Cullen," Dorety said, "you are in command of this ship, and it is not proper for me to comment now upon what you do. But I wish to say one thing. There is a hereafter, and yours will be a hot one."

Captain Cullen did not even scowl. In his voice was regret as he said:—"It was blowing a living gale. It was impossible to save the man."

"He fell from the royal-yard," Dorety cried hotly. "You were setting the royals at the time. Fifteen minutes afterward you were setting the skysails."

"It was a living gale, wasn't it, Mr. Higgins?" Captain Cullen said, turning to the mate.

"If you'd brought her to, it'd have taken the sticks out of her," was the mate's answer. "You did the proper thing, Captain Cullen. The man hadn't a ghost of a show."

George Dorety made no answer, and to the meal's end no one spoke. After that, Dorety had his meals served in his stateroom. Captain Cullen scowled at him no longer, though no speech was exchanged between them, while the Mary Rogers sped north toward warmer latitudes. At the end of the week, Dan Cullen cornered Dorety on deck.

"What are you going to do when we get to Frisco?" he demanded bluntly.

"I am going to swear out a warrant for your arrest," Dorety answered quietly. "I am going to charge you with murder, and I am going to see you hanged for it."

"You're almighty sure of yourself," Captain Cullen sneered, turning on his heel.

A second week passed, and one morning found George Dorety standing in the coach-house companionway at the for'ard end of the long poop, taking his first gaze around the deck. The Mary Rogers was reaching full-and-by, in a stiff breeze. Every sail was set and drawing, including the staysails. Captain Cullen strolled for'ard along the poop. He strolled carelessly, glancing at the passenger out of the corner of his eye. Dorety was looking the other way, standing with head and shoulders outside the companionway, and only the back of his head was to be seen. Captain Cullen, with swift eye, embraced the mainstaysail-block and the head and estimated the distance. He glanced about him. Nobody was looking. Aft, Joshua Higgins, pacing up and down, had just turned his back and was going the other way. Captain Cullen bent over suddenly and cast the staysail-sheet off from its pin. The heavy block hurtled through the air, smashing Dorety's head like an egg-shell and hurtling on and back and forth as the staysail whipped and slatted in the wind. Joshua Higgins turned around to see what had carried away, and met the full blast of the vilest portion of Captain Cullen's profanity.

"I made the sheet fast myself," whimpered the mate in the first lull, "with an extra turn to make sure. I remember it distinctly."

"Made fast?" the captain snarled back, for the benefit of the watch as it struggled to capture the flying sail before it tore to ribbons. "You couldn't make your grandmother fast, you useless scullion. If you made that sheet fast with an extra turn, why didn't it stay fast? That's what I want to know. Why didn't it stay fast?"

The mate whined inarticulately.

"Oh, shut up!" was the final word of Captain Cullen.

Half an hour later he was as surprised as any when the body of George Dorety was found inside the companionway on the floor. In the afternoon, alone in his room, he doctored up the log.

"Ordinary seaman, Karl Brun," he wrote, "lost overboard from foreroyal-yard in a gale of wind. Was running at the time, and for the safety of the ship did not dare come up to the wind. Nor could a boat have lived in the sea that was running."

On another page, he wrote:—

"Had often warned Mr. Dorety about the danger he ran because of his carelessness on deck. I told him, once, that some day he would get his head knocked off by a block. A carelessly fastened mainstaysail sheet was the cause of the accident, which was deeply to be regretted because Mr. Dorety was a favorite with all of us."

Captain Dan Cullen read over his literary effort with admiration, blotted the page, and closed the log. He lighted a cigar and stared before him. He felt the Mary Rogers lift, and heel, and surge along, and knew that she was making nine knots. A smile of satisfaction slowly dawned on his black and hairy face. Well, anyway, he had made his westing and fooled God.

THE HEATHEN

I met him first in a hurricane; and though we had gone through the hurricane on the same schooner, it was not until the schooner had gone to pieces under us that I first laid eyes on him. Without doubt I had seen him with the rest of the kanaka crew on board, but I had not consciously been aware of his existence, for the Petite Jeanne was rather overcrowded. In addition to her eight or ten kanaka seamen, her white captain, mate, and supercargo, and her six cabin passengers, she sailed from Rangiroa with something like eighty-five deck passengers—Paumotans and Tahitians, men, women, and children each with a trade box, to say nothing of sleeping-mats, blankets, and clothes-bundles.

The pearling season in the Paumotus was over, and all hands were returning to Tahiti. The six of us cabin passengers were pearl-buyers. Two were Americans, one was Ah Choon (the whitest Chinese I have ever known), one was a German, one was a Polish Jew, and I completed the half dozen.

It had been a prosperous season. Not one of us had cause for complaint, nor one of the eighty-five deck passengers either. All had done well, and all were looking forward to a rest-off and a good time in Papeete.

Of course, the Petite Jeanne was overloaded. She was only seventy tons, and she had no right to carry a tithe of the mob she had on board. Beneath her hatches she was crammed and jammed with pearl-shell and copra. Even the trade room was packed full of shell. It was a miracle that the sailors could work her. There was no moving about the decks. They simply climbed back and forth along the rails.

In the night-time they walked upon the sleepers, who carpeted the deck, I'll swear, two deep. Oh! and there were pigs and chickens on deck, and sacks of yams, while every conceivable place was festooned with strings of drinking cocoanuts and bunches of bananas. On both sides, between the fore and main shrouds, guys had been stretched, just low enough for the foreboom to swing clear; and from each of these guys at least fifty bunches of bananas were suspended.

It promised to be a messy passage, even if we did make it in the two or three days that would have been required if the southeast trades had been blowing fresh. But they weren't blowing fresh. After the first five hours the trade died away in a dozen or so gasping fans. The calm continued all that night and the next day—one of those glaring, glassy calms, when the very thought of opening one's eyes to look at it is sufficient to cause a headache.

The second day a man died—an Easter Islander, one of the best divers that season in the lagoon. Smallpox—that is what it was; though how smallpox could come on board, when there had been no known cases ashore when we left Rangiroa, is beyond me. There it was, though—smallpox, a man dead, and three others down on their backs.

There was nothing to be done. We could not segregate the sick, nor could we care for them. We were packed like sardines. There was nothing to do but rot or die—that is, there was nothing to do after the night that followed the first death. On that night, the mate, the supercargo, the Polish Jew, and four native divers sneaked away in the large whale-boat. They were never heard of again. In the morning the captain promptly scuttled the remaining boats, and there we were.

That day there were two deaths; the following day three; then it jumped to eight. It was curious to see how we took it. The natives, for instance, fell into a condition of dumb, stolid fear. The captain—Oudouse, his name was, a Frenchman—became very nervous and voluble. He actually got the twitches. He was a large, fleshy man, weighing at least two hundred pounds, and he quickly became a faithful representation of a quivering jelly-mountain of fat.

The German, the two Americans, and myself bought up all the Scotch whiskey, and proceeded to stay drunk. The theory was beautiful—namely, if we kept ourselves soaked in alcohol, every smallpox germ that came into contact with us would immediately be scorched to a cinder. And the theory worked, though I must confess that neither Captain Oudouse nor Ah Choon were attacked by the disease either. The Frenchman did not drink at all, while Ah Choon restricted himself to one drink daily.

It was a pretty time. The sun, going into northern declination, was straight overhead. There was no wind, except for frequent squalls, which blew fiercely for from five minutes to half an hour, and wound up by deluging us with rain. After each squall, the awful sun would come out, drawing clouds of steam from the soaked decks.

The steam was not nice. It was the vapor of death, freighted with millions and millions of germs. We always took another drink when we saw it going up from the dead and dying, and usually we took two or three more drinks, mixing them exceptionally stiff. Also, we made it a rule to take an additional several each time they hove the dead over to the sharks that swarmed about us.

We had a week of it, and then the whiskey gave out. It is just as well, or I shouldn't be alive now. It took a sober man to pull through what followed, as you will see when I mention the little fact that only two men did pull through. The other man was the heathen—at least, that was what I heard Captain Oudouse call him at the moment I first became aware of the heathen's existence. But to come back.

It was at the end of the week, with the whiskey gone, and the pearl-buyers sober, that I happened to glance at the barometer that hung in the cabin companionway. Its normal register in the Paumotus was 29.90, and it was quite customary to see it vacillate between 29.85 and 30.00, or even 30.05; but to see it as I saw it, down to 29.62, was sufficient to sober the most drunken pearl-buyer that ever incinerated smallpox microbes in Scotch whiskey.

I called Captain Oudouse's attention to it, only to be informed that he had watched it going down for several hours. There was little to do, but that little he did very well, considering the circumstances. He took off the light sails, shortened right down to storm canvas, spread life-lines, and waited for the wind. His mistake lay in what he did after the wind came. He hove to on the port tack, which was the right thing to do south of the Equator, if—and there was the rub—if one were not in the direct path of the hurricane.

We were in the direct path. I could see that by the steady increase of the wind and the equally steady fall of the barometer. I wanted him to turn and run with the wind on the port quarter until the barometer ceased falling, and then to heave to. We argued till he was reduced to hysteria, but budge he would not. The worst of it was that I could not get the rest of the pearl-buyers to back me up. Who was I, anyway, to know more about the sea and its ways than a properly qualified captain? was what was in their minds, I knew.

Of course the sea rose with the wind frightfully; and I shall never forget the first three seas the Petite Jeanne shipped. She had fallen off, as vessels do at times when hove to, and the first sea made a clean breach. The life-lines were only for the strong and well, and little good were they even for them when the women and children, the bananas and cocoanuts, the pigs and trade boxes, the sick and the dying, were swept along in a solid, screeching, groaning mass.

The second sea filled the Petite Jeanne's decks flush with the rails; and, as her stern sank down and her bow tossed skyward, all the miserable dunnage of life and luggage poured aft. It was a human torrent. They came head-first, feet-first, sidewise, rolling over and over, twisting, squirming, writhing, and crumpling up.

Now and again one caught a grip on a stanchion or a rope; but the weight of the bodies behind tore such grips loose.

One man I noticed fetch up, head on and square on, with the starboard-bitt. His head cracked like an egg. I saw what was coming, sprang on top of the cabin, and from there into the mainsail itself. Ah Choon and one of the Americans tried to follow me, but I was one jump ahead of them. The American was swept away and over the stern like a piece of chaff. Ah Choon caught a spoke of the wheel, and swung in behind it. But a strapping Raratonga vahine (woman)—she must have weighed two hundred and fifty—brought up against him, and got an arm around his neck. He clutched the kanaka steersman with his other hand; and just at that moment the schooner flung down to starboard.

The rush of bodies and sea that was coming along the port runway between the cabin and the rail turned abruptly and poured to starboard. Away they went—vahine, Ah Choon, and steersman: and I swear I saw Ah Choon grin at me with philosophic resignation as he cleared the rail and went under.

The third sea—the biggest of the three—did not do so much damage. By the time it arrived nearly everybody was in the rigging. On deck perhaps a dozen gasping, half-drowned, and half-stunned wretches were rolling about or attempting to crawl into safety. They went by the board, as did the wreckage of the two remaining boats. The other pearl-buyers and myself, between seas, managed to get about fifteen women and children into the cabin, and battened down. Little good it did the poor creatures in the end.

Wind? Out of all my experience I could not have believed it possible for the wind to blow as it did. There is no describing it. How can one describe a nightmare? It was the same way with that wind. It tore the clothes off our bodies. I say tore them off, and I mean it. I am not asking you to believe it. I am merely telling something that I saw and felt. There are times when I do not believe it myself. I went through it, and that is enough. One could not face that wind and live. It was a monstrous thing, and the most monstrous thing about it was that it increased and continued to increase.

Imagine countless millions and billions of tons of sand. Imagine this sand tearing along at ninety, a hundred, a hundred and twenty, or any other number of miles per hour. Imagine, further, this sand to be invisible, impalpable, yet to retain all the weight and density of sand. Do all this, and you may get a vague inkling of what that wind was like.

Perhaps sand is not the right comparison. Consider it mud, invisible, impalpable, but heavy as mud. Nay, it goes beyond that. Consider every molecule of air to be a mud-bank in itself. Then try to imagine the multitudinous impact of mud-banks. No; it is beyond me. Language may be adequate to express the ordinary conditions of life, but it cannot possibly express any of the conditions of so enormous a blast of wind. It would have been better had I stuck by my original intention of not attempting a description.

I will say this much: The sea, which had risen at first, was beaten down by that wind. More: it seemed as if the whole ocean had been sucked up in the maw of the hurricane, and hurled on through that portion of space which previously had been occupied by the air.

Of course, our canvas had gone long before. But Captain Oudouse had on the Petite Jeanne something I had never before seen on a South Sea schooner—a sea-anchor. It was a conical canvas bag, the mouth of which was kept open by a huge hoop of iron. The sea-anchor was bridled something like a kite, so that it bit into the water as a kite bites into the air, but with a difference. The sea-anchor remained just under the surface of the ocean in a perpendicular position. A long line, in turn, connected it with the schooner. As a result, the Petite Jeanne rode bow on to the wind and to what sea there was.

The situation really would have been favorable had we not been in the path of the storm. True, the wind itself tore our canvas out of the gaskets, jerked out our topmasts, and made a raffle of our running-gear, but still we would have come through nicely had we not been square in front of the advancing storm-centre. That was what fixed us. I was in a state of stunned, numbed, paralyzed collapse from enduring the impact of the wind, and I think I was just about ready to give up and die when the centre smote us. The blow we received was an absolute lull. There was not a breath of air. The effect on one was sickening.

Remember that for hours we had been at terrific muscular tension, withstanding the awful pressure of that wind. And then, suddenly, the pressure was removed. I know that I felt as though I was about to expand, to fly apart in all directions. It seemed as if every atom composing my body was repelling every other atom and was on the verge of rushing off irresistibly into space. But that lasted only for a moment. Destruction was upon us.

In the absence of the wind and pressure the sea rose. It jumped, it leaped, it soared straight toward the clouds. Remember, from every point of the compass that inconceivable wind was blowing in toward the centre of calm. The result was that the seas sprang up from every point of the compass. There was no wind to check them. They popped up like corks released from the bottom of a pail of water. There was no system to them, no stability. They were hollow, maniacal seas. They were eighty feet high at the least. They were not seas at all. They resembled no sea a man had ever seen.

They were splashes, monstrous splashes—that is all. Splashes that were eighty feet high. Eighty! They were more than eighty. They went over our mastheads. They were spouts, explosions. They were drunken. They fell anywhere, anyhow. They jostled one another; they collided. They rushed together and collapsed upon one another, or fell apart like a thousand waterfalls all at once. It was no ocean any man had ever dreamed of, that hurricane centre. It was confusion thrice confounded. It was anarchy. It was a hell-pit of sea-water gone mad.

The Petite Jeanne? I don't know. The heathen told me afterward that he did not know. She was literally torn apart, ripped wide open, beaten into a pulp, smashed into kindling wood, annihilated. When I came to I was in the water, swimming automatically, though I was about two-thirds drowned. How I got there I had no recollection. I remembered seeing the Petite Jeanne fly to pieces at what must have been the instant that my own consciousness was buffetted out of me. But there I was, with nothing to do but make the best of it, and in that best there was little promise. The wind was blowing again, the sea was much smaller and more regular, and I knew that I had passed through the centre. Fortunately, there were no sharks about. The hurricane had dissipated the ravenous horde that had surrounded the death ship and fed off the dead.

It was about midday when the Petite Jeanne went to pieces, and it must have been two hours afterward when I picked up with one of her hatch-covers. Thick rain was driving at the time; and it was the merest chance that flung me and the hatch-cover together. A short length of line was trailing from the rope handle; and I knew that I was good for a day, at least, if the sharks did not return. Three hours later, possibly a little longer, sticking close to the cover, and, with closed eyes, concentrating my whole soul upon the task of breathing in enough air to keep me going and at the same time of avoiding breathing in enough water to drown me, it seemed to me that I heard voices. The rain had ceased, and wind and sea were easing marvellously. Not twenty feet away from me on another hatch-cover, were Captain Oudouse and the heathen. They were fighting over the possession of the cover—at least, the Frenchman was.

"Paien noir!" I heard him scream, and at the same time I saw him kick the kanaka.

Now, Captain Oudouse had lost all his clothes, except his shoes, and they were heavy brogans. It was a cruel blow, for it caught the heathen on the mouth and the point of the chin, half stunning him. I looked for him to retaliate, but he contented himself with swimming about forlornly a safe ten feet away. Whenever a fling of the sea threw him closer, the Frenchman, hanging on with his hands, kicked out at him with both feet. Also, at the moment of delivering each kick, he called the kanaka a black heathen.

"For two centimes I'd come over there and drown you, you white beast!" I yelled.

The only reason I did not go was that I felt too tired. The very thought of the effort to swim over was nauseating. So I called to the kanaka to come to me, and proceeded to share the hatch-cover with him. Otoo, he told me his name was (pronounced o-to-o); also, he told me that he was a native of Bora Bora, the most westerly of the Society Group. As I learned afterward, he had got the hatch-cover first, and, after some time, encountering Captain Oudouse, had offered to share it with him, and had been kicked off for his pains.

And that was how Otoo and I first came together. He was no fighter. He was all sweetness and gentleness, a love-creature, though he stood nearly six feet tall and was muscled like a gladiator. He was no fighter, but he was also no coward. He had the heart of a lion; and in the years that followed I have seen him run risks that I would never dream of taking. What I mean is that while he was no fighter, and while he always avoided precipitating a row, he never ran away from trouble when it started. And it was "'Ware shoal!" when once Otoo went into action. I shall never forget what he did to Bill King. It occurred in German Samoa. Bill King was hailed the champion heavyweight of the American Navy. He was a big brute of a man, a veritable gorilla, one of those hard-hitting, rough-housing chaps, and clever with his fists as well. He picked the quarrel, and he kicked Otoo twice and struck him once before Otoo felt it to be necessary to fight. I don't think it lasted four minutes, at the end of which time Bill King was the unhappy possessor of four broken ribs, a broken forearm, and a dislocated shoulder-blade. Otoo knew nothing of scientific boxing. He was merely a manhandler; and Bill King was something like three months in recovering from the bit of manhandling he received that afternoon on Apia beach.

But I am running ahead of my yarn. We shared the hatch-cover between us. We took turn and turn about, one lying flat on the cover and resting, while the other, submerged to the neck, merely held on with his hands. For two days and nights, spell and spell, on the cover and in the water, we drifted over the ocean. Toward the last I was delirious most of the time; and there were times, too, when I heard Otoo babbling and raving in his native tongue. Our continuous immersion prevented us from dying of thirst, though the sea-water and the sunshine gave us the prettiest imaginable combination of salt pickle and sunburn.

In the end, Otoo saved my life; for I came to lying on the beach twenty feet from the water, sheltered from the sun by a couple of cocoanut leaves. No one but Otoo could have dragged me there and stuck up the leaves for shade. He was lying beside me. I went off again; and the next time I came round, it was cool and starry night, and Otoo was pressing a drinking cocoanut to my lips.

We were the sole survivors of the Petite Jeanne. Captain Oudouse must have succumbed to exhaustion, for several days later his hatch-cover drifted ashore without him. Otoo and I lived with the natives of the atoll for a week, when we were rescued by a French cruiser and taken to Tahiti. In the meantime, however, we had performed the ceremony of exchanging names. In the South Seas such a ceremony binds two men closer together than blood-brothership. The initiative had been mine; and Otoo was rapturously delighted when I suggested it.

"It is well," he said, in Tahitian. "For we have been mates together for two days on the lips of Death."

"But Death stuttered." I smiled.

"It was a brave deed you did, master," he replied, "and Death was not vile enough to speak."

"Why do you 'master' me?" I demanded, with a show of hurt feelings. "We have exchanged names. To you I am Otoo. To me you are Charley. And between you and me, forever and forever, you shall be Charley, and I shall be Otoo. It is the way of the custom. And when we die, if it does happen that we live again somewhere beyond the stars and the sky, still shall you be Charley to me, and I Otoo to you."

"Yes, master," he answered, his eyes luminous and soft with joy.

"There you go!" I cried indignantly.

"What does it matter what my lips utter?" he argued. "They are only my lips. But I shall think Otoo always. Whenever I think of myself, I shall think of you. Whenever men call me by name, I shall think of you. And beyond the sky and beyond the stars, always and forever, you shall be Otoo to me. Is it well, master?"

I hid my smile, and answered that it was well.

We parted at Papeete. I remained ashore to recuperate; and he went on in a cutter to his own island, Bora Bora. Six weeks later he was back. I was surprised, for he had told me of his wife, and said that he was returning to her, and would give over sailing on far voyages.

"Where do you go, master?" he asked after our first greetings.

I shrugged my shoulders. It was a hard question.

"All the world," was my answer—"all the world, all the sea, and all the islands that are in the sea."

"I will go with you," he said simply. "My wife is dead."

I never had a brother; but from what I have seen of other men's brothers, I doubt if any man ever had a brother that was to him what Otoo was to me. He was brother and father and mother as well. And this I know: I lived a straighter and better man because of Otoo. I cared little for other men, but I had to live straight in Otoo's eyes. Because of him I dared not tarnish myself. He made me his ideal, compounding me, I fear, chiefly out of his own love and worship; and there were times when I stood close to the steep pitch of Hades, and would have taken the plunge had not the thought of Otoo restrained me. His pride in me entered into me, until it became one of the major rules in my personal code to do nothing that would diminish that pride of his.

Naturally, I did not learn right away what his feelings were toward me. He never criticised, never censured; and slowly the exalted place I held in his eyes dawned upon me, and slowly I grew to comprehend the hurt I could inflict upon him by being anything less than my best.

For seventeen years we were together; for seventeen years he was at my shoulder, watching while I slept, nursing me through fever and wounds—ay, and receiving wounds in fighting for me. He signed on the same ships with me; and together we ranged the Pacific from Hawaii to Sydney Head, and from Torres Straits to the Galapagos. We blackbirded from the New Hebrides and the Line Islands over to the westward clear through the Louisades, New Britain, New Ireland, and New Hanover. We were wrecked three times—in the Gilberts, in the Santa Cruz group, and in the Fijis. And we traded and salved wherever a dollar promised in the way of pearl and pearl-shell, copra, beche-de-mer, hawkbill turtle-shell, and stranded wrecks.

It began in Papeete, immediately after his announcement that he was going with me over all the sea, and the islands in the midst thereof. There was a club in those days in Papeete, where the pearlers, traders, captains, and riffraff of South Sea adventurers foregathered. The play ran high, and the drink ran high; and I am very much afraid that I kept later hours than were becoming or proper. No matter what the hour was when I left the club, there was Otoo waiting to see me safely home.

At first I smiled; next I chided him. Then I told him flatly that I stood in need of no wet-nursing. After that I did not see him when I came out of the club. Quite by accident, a week or so later, I discovered that he still saw me home, lurking across the street among the shadows of the mango-trees. What could I do? I know what I did do.

Insensibly I began to keep better hours. On wet and stormy nights, in the thick of the folly and the fun, the thought would persist in coming to me of Otoo keeping his dreary vigil under the dripping mangoes. Truly, he had made a better man of me. Yet he was not strait-laced. And he knew nothing of common Christian morality. All the people on Bora Bora were Christians; but he was a heathen, the only unbeliever on the island, a gross materialist, who believed that when he died he was dead. He believed merely in fair play and square dealing. Petty meanness, in his code, was almost as serious as wanton homicide; and I do believe that he respected a murderer more than a man given to small practices.

Otoo had my welfare always at heart. He thought ahead for me, weighed my plans, and took a greater interest in them than I did myself. At first, when I was unaware of this interest of his in my affairs, he had to divine my intentions, as, for instance, at Papeete, when I contemplated going partners with a knavish fellow-countryman on a guano venture. I did not know he was a knave. Nor did any white man in Papeete. Neither did Otoo know, but he saw how thick we were getting, and found out for me, and without my asking him. Native sailors from the ends of the seas knock about on the beach in Tahiti; and Otoo, suspicious merely, went among them till he had gathered sufficient data to justify his suspicions. Oh, it was a nice history, that of Randolph Waters. I couldn't believe it when Otoo first narrated it; but when I sheeted it home to Waters he gave in without a murmur, and got away on the first steamer to Aukland.

At first, I am free to confess, I couldn't help resenting Otoo's poking his nose into my business. But I knew that he was wholly unselfish; and soon I had to acknowledge his wisdom and discretion. He had his eyes open always to my main chance, and he was both keen-sighted and far-sighted. In time he became my counsellor, until he knew more of my business than I did myself. He really had my interest at heart more than I did. Mine was the magnificent carelessness of youth, for I preferred romance to dollars, and adventure to a comfortable billet with all night in. So it was well that I had some one to look out for me. I know that if it had not been for Otoo, I should not be here to-day.

Of numerous instances, let me give one. I had had some experience in blackbirding before I went pearling in the Paumotus. Otoo and I were in Samoa—we really were on the beach and hard aground—when my chance came to go as recruiter on a blackbird brig. Otoo signed on before the mast; and for the next half-dozen years, in as many ships, we knocked about the wildest portions of Melanesia. Otoo saw to it that he always pulled stroke-oar in my boat. Our custom in recruiting labor was to land the recruiter on the beach. The covering boat always lay on its oars several hundred feet off shore, while the recruiter's boat, also lying on its oars, kept afloat on the edge of the beach. When I landed with my trade-goods, leaving my steering sweep apeak, Otoo left his stroke position and came into the stern-sheets, where a Winchester lay ready to hand under a flap of canvas. The boat's crew was also armed, the Sniders concealed under canvas flaps that ran the length of the gunwales. While I was busy arguing and persuading the woolly-headed cannibals to come and labor on the Queensland plantations Otoo kept watch. And often and often his low voice warned me of suspicious actions and impending treachery. Sometimes it was the quick shot from his rifle, knocking a savage over, that was the first warning I received. And in my rush to the boat his hand was always there to jerk me flying aboard. Once, I remember, on Santa Anna, the boat grounded just as the trouble began. The covering boat was dashing to our assistance, but the several score of savages would have wiped us out before it arrived. Otoo took a flying leap ashore, dug both hands into the trade-goods, and scattered tobacco, beads, tomahawks, knives, and calicoes in all directions.

This was too much for the woolly-heads. While they scrambled for the treasures, the boat was shoved clear, and we were aboard and forty feet away. And I got thirty recruits off that very beach in the next four hours.

The particular instance I have in mind was on Malaita, the most savage island in the easterly Solomons. The natives had been remarkably friendly; and how were we to know that the whole village had been taking up a collection for over two years with which to buy a white man's head? The beggars are all head-hunters, and they especially esteem a white man's head. The fellow who captured the head would receive the whole collection. As I say, they appeared very friendly; and on this day I was fully a hundred yards down the beach from the boat. Otoo had cautioned me; and, as usual when I did not heed him, I came to grief.

The first I knew, a cloud of spears sailed out of the mangrove swamp at me. At least a dozen were sticking into me. I started to run, but tripped over one that was fast in my calf, and went down. The woolly-heads made a run for me, each with a long-handled, fantail tomahawk with which to hack off my head. They were so eager for the prize that they got in one another's way. In the confusion, I avoided several hacks by throwing myself right and left on the sand.

Then Otoo arrived—Otoo the manhandler. In some way he had got hold of a heavy war club, and at close quarters it was a far more efficient weapon than a rifle. He was right in the thick of them, so that they could not spear him, while their tomahawks seemed worse than useless. He was fighting for me, and he was in a true Berserker rage. The way he handled that club was amazing. Their skulls squashed like overripe oranges. It was not until he had driven them back, picked me up in his arms, and started to run, that he received his first wounds. He arrived in the boat with four spear thrusts, got his Winchester, and with it got a man for every shot. Then we pulled aboard the schooner and doctored up.

Seventeen years we were together. He made me. I should to-day be a supercargo, a recruiter, or a memory, if it had not been for him.

"You spend your money, and you go out and get more," he said one day. "It is easy to get money now. But when you get old, your money will be spent, and you will not be able to go out and get more. I know, master. I have studied the way of white men. On the beaches are many old men who were young once, and who could get money just like you. Now they are old, and they have nothing, and they wait about for the young men like you to come ashore and buy drinks for them.

"The black boy is a slave on the plantations. He gets twenty dollars a year. He works hard. The overseer does not work hard. He rides a horse and watches the black boy work. He gets twelve hundred dollars a year. I am a sailor on the schooner. I get fifteen dollars a month. That is because I am a good sailor. I work hard. The captain has a double awning, and drinks beer out of long bottles. I have never seen him haul a rope or pull an oar. He gets one hundred and fifty dollars a month. I am a sailor. He is a navigator. Master, I think it would be very good for you to know navigation."

Otoo spurred me on to it. He sailed with me as second mate

on my first schooner, and he was far prouder of my command than I was myself. Later on it was:

"The captain is well paid, master; but the ship is in his keeping, and he is never free from the burden. It is the owner who is better paid—the owner who sits ashore with many servants and turns his money over."

"True, but a schooner costs five thousand dollars—an old schooner at that," I objected. "I should be an old man before I saved five thousand dollars."

"There be short ways for white men to make money," he went on, pointing ashore at the cocoanut-fringed beach.

We were in the Solomons at the time, picking up a cargo of ivory-nuts along the east coast of Guadalcanar.

"Between this river mouth and the next it is two miles," he said. "The flat land runs far back. It is worth nothing now. Next year—who knows?—or the year after, men will pay much money for that land. The anchorage is good. Big steamers can lie close up. You can buy the land four miles deep from the old chief for ten thousand sticks of tobacco, ten bottles of square-face, and a Snider, which will cost you, maybe, one hundred dollars. Then you place the deed with the commissioner; and the next year, or the year after, you sell and become the owner of a ship."

I followed his lead, and his words came true, though in three years, instead of two. Next came the grasslands deal on Guadalcanar—twenty thousand acres, on a governmental nine hundred and ninety-nine years' lease at a nominal sum. I owned the lease for precisely ninety days, when I sold it to a company for half a fortune. Always it was Otoo who looked ahead and saw the opportunity. He was responsible for the salving of the Doncaster—bought in at auction for a hundred pounds, and clearing three thousand after every expense was paid. He led me into the Savaii plantation and the cocoa venture on Upolu.

We did not go seafaring so much as in the old days. I was too well off. I married, and my standard of living rose; but Otoo remained the same old-time Otoo, moving about the house or trailing through the office, his wooden pipe in his mouth, a shilling undershirt on his back, and a four-shilling lava-lava about his loins. I could not get him to spend money. There was no way of repaying him except with love, and God knows he got that in full measure from all of us. The children worshipped him; and if he had been spoilable, my wife would surely have been his undoing.

The children! He really was the one who showed them the way of their feet in the world practical. He began by teaching them to walk. He sat up with them when they were sick. One by one, when they were scarcely toddlers, he took them down to the lagoon, and made them into amphibians. He taught them more than I ever knew of the habits of fish and the ways of catching them. In the bush it was the same thing. At seven, Tom knew more woodcraft than I ever dreamed existed. At six, Mary went over the Sliding Rock without a quiver, and I have seen strong men balk at that feat. And when Frank had just turned six he could bring up shillings from the bottom in three fathoms.

"My people in Bora Bora do not like heathen—they are all Christians; and I do not like Bora Bora Christians," he said one day, when I, with the idea of getting him to spend some of the money that was rightfully his, had been trying to persuade him to make a visit to his own island in one of our schooners—a special voyage which I had hoped to make a record breaker in the matter of prodigal expense.

I say one of our schooners, though legally at the time they belonged to me. I struggled long with him to enter into partnership.

"We have been partners from the day the Petite Jeanne went down," he said at last. "But if your heart so wishes, then shall we become partners by the law. I have no work to do, yet are my expenses large. I drink and eat and smoke in plenty—it costs much, I know. I do not pay for the playing of billiards, for I play on your table; but still the money goes. Fishing on the reef is only a rich man's pleasure. It is shocking, the cost of hooks and cotton line. Yes; it is necessary that we be partners by the law. I need the money. I shall get it from the head clerk in the office."

So the papers were made out and recorded. A year later I was compelled to complain.

"Charley," said I, "you are a wicked old fraud, a miserly skinflint, a miserable land-crab. Behold, your share for the year in all our partnership has been thousands of dollars. The head clerk has given me this paper. It says that in the year you have drawn just eighty-seven dollars and twenty cents."

"Is there any owing me?" he asked anxiously.

"I tell you thousands and thousands," I answered.

His face brightened, as with an immense relief.

"It is well," he said. "See that the head clerk keeps good account of it. When I want it, I shall want it, and there must not be a cent missing.

"If there is," he added fiercely, after a pause, "it must come out of the clerk's wages."

And all the time, as I afterward learned, his will, drawn up by

Carruthers, and making me sole beneficiary, lay in the American consul's safe.

But the end came, as the end must come to all human associations. It occurred in the Solomons, where our wildest work had been done in the wild young days, and where we were once more—principally on a holiday, incidentally to look after our holdings on Florida Island and to look over the pearling possibilities of the Mboli Pass. We were lying at Savo, having run in to trade for curios.

Now, Savo is alive with sharks. The custom of the woolly-heads of burying their dead in the sea did not tend to discourage the sharks from making the adjacent waters a hang-out. It was my luck to be coming aboard in a tiny, overloaded, native canoe, when the thing capsized. There were four woolly-heads and myself in it, or, rather, hanging to it. The schooner was a hundred yards away. I was just hailing for a boat when one of the woolly-heads began to scream. Holding on to the end of the canoe, both he and that portion of the canoe were dragged under several times. Then he loosed his clutch and disappeared. A shark had got him.

The three remaining savages tried to climb out of the water upon the bottom of the canoe. I yelled and struck at the nearest with my fist, but it was no use. They were in a blind funk. The canoe could barely have supported one of them. Under the three it upended and rolled sidewise, throwing them back into the water.

I abandoned the canoe and started to swim toward the schooner, expecting to be picked up by the boat before I got there. One of the savages elected to come with me, and we swam along silently, side by side, now and again putting our faces into the water and peering about for sharks. The screams of the man who stayed by the canoe informed us that he was taken. I was peering into the water when I saw a big shark pass directly beneath me. He was fully sixteen feet in length. I saw the whole thing. He got the woolly-head by the middle, and away he went, the poor devil, head, shoulders, and arms out of water all the time, screeching in a heartrending way. He was carried along in this fashion for several hundred feet, when he was dragged beneath the surface.

I swam doggedly on, hoping that that was the last unattached shark. But there was another. Whether it was the one that had attacked the natives earlier, or whether it was one that had made a good meal elsewhere, I do not know. At any rate, he was not in such haste as the others. I could not swim so rapidly now, for a large part of my effort was devoted to keeping track of him. I was watching him when he made his first attack. By good luck I got both hands on his nose, and, though his momentum nearly shoved me under, I managed to keep him off. He veered clear, and began circling about again. A second time I escaped him by the same maneuver. The third rush was a miss on both sides. He sheered at the moment my hands should have landed on his nose, but his sandpaper hide (I had on a sleeveless undershirt) scraped the skin off one arm from elbow to shoulder.

By this time I was played out, and gave up hope. The schooner was still two hundred feet away. My face was in the water, and I was watching him maneuver for another attempt, when I saw a brown body pass between us. It was Otoo.

"Swim for the schooner, master!" he said. And he spoke gayly, as though the affair was a mere lark. "I know sharks. The shark is my brother."

I obeyed, swimming slowly on, while Otoo swam about me, keeping always between me and the shark, foiling his rushes and encouraging me.

"The davit tackle carried away, and they are rigging the falls," he explained, a minute or so later, and then went under to head off another attack.

By the time the schooner was thirty feet away I was about done for. I could scarcely move. They were heaving lines at us from on board, but they continually fell short. The shark, finding that it was receiving no hurt, had become bolder. Several times it nearly got me, but each time Otoo was there just the moment before it was too late. Of course, Otoo could have saved himself any time. But he stuck by me.

"Good-bye, Charley! I'm finished!" I just managed to gasp.

I knew that the end had come, and that the next moment I should throw up my hands and go down.

But Otoo laughed in my face, saying:

"I will show you a new trick. I will make that shark feel sick!"

He dropped in behind me, where the shark was preparing to come at me.

"A little more to the left!" he next called out. "There is a line there on the water. To the left, master—to the left!"

I changed my course and struck out blindly. I was by that time barely conscious. As my hand closed on the line I heard an exclamation from on board. I turned and looked. There was no sign of Otoo. The next instant he broke surface. Both hands were off at the wrist, the stumps spouting blood.

"Otoo!" he called softly. And I could see in his gaze the love that thrilled in his voice.

Then, and then only, at the very last of all our years, he called me by that name.

"Good-by, Otoo!" he called.

Then he was dragged under, and I was hauled aboard, where I fainted in the captain's arms.

And so passed Otoo, who saved me and made me a man, and who saved me in the end. We met in the maw of a hurricane, and parted in the maw of a shark, with seventeen intervening years of comradeship, the like of which I dare to assert has never befallen two men, the one brown and the other white. If Jehovah be from His high place watching every sparrow fall, not least in His kingdom shall be Otoo, the one heathen of Bora Bora.

THE HOBO AND THE FAIRY

He lay on his back. So heavy was his sleep that the stamp of hoofs and cries of the drivers from the bridge that crossed the creek did not rouse him. Wagon after wagon, loaded high with grapes, passed the bridge on the way up the valley to the winery, and the coming of each wagon was like the explosion of sound and commotion in the lazy quiet of the afternoon.

But the man was undisturbed. His head had slipped from the folded newspaper, and the straggling, unkempt hair was matted with the foxtails and burrs of the dry grass on which it lay. He was not a pretty sight. His mouth was open, disclosing a gap in the upper row where several teeth at some time had been knocked out. He breathed stertorously, at times grunting and moaning with the pain of his sleep. Also, he was very restless, tossing his arms about, making jerky, half-convulsive movements, and at times rolling his head from side to side in the burrs. This restlessness seemed occasioned partly by some internal discomfort, and partly by the sun that streamed down on his face and by the flies that buzzed and lighted and crawled upon the nose and cheeks and eyelids. There was no other place for them to crawl, for the rest of the face was covered with matted beard, slightly grizzled, but greatly dirt-stained and weather-discolored.

The cheek-bones were blotched with the blood congested by the debauch that was evidently being slept off. This, too, accounted for the persistence with which the flies clustered around the mouth, lured by the alcohol-laden exhalations. He was a powerfully built man, thick-necked, broad-shouldered, with sinewy wrists and toil-distorted hands. Yet the distortion was not due to recent toil, nor were the callouses other than ancient that showed under the dirt of the one palm upturned. From time to time this hand clenched tightly and spasmodically into a fist, large, heavy-boned and wicked-looking.

The man lay in the dry grass of a tiny glade that ran down to the tree-fringed bank of the stream. On either side of the glade was a fence, of the old stake-and-rider type, though little of it was to be seen, so thickly was it overgrown by wild blackberry bushes, scrubby oaks and young madrono trees. In the rear, a gate through a low paling fence led to a snug, squat bungalow, built in the California Spanish style and seeming to have been compounded directly from the landscape of which it was so justly a part. Neat and trim and modestly sweet was the bungalow, redolent of comfort and repose, telling with quiet certitude of some one that knew, and that had sought and found.

Through the gate and into the glade came as dainty a little maiden as ever stepped out of an illustration made especially to show how dainty little maidens may be. Eight years she might have been, and, possibly, a trifle more, or less. Her little waist and little black-stockinged calves showed how delicately fragile she was; but the fragility was of mould only. There was no hint of anemia in the clear, healthy complexion nor in the quick, tripping step. She was a little, delicious blond, with hair spun of gossamer gold and wide blue eyes that were but slightly veiled by the long lashes. Her expression was of sweetness and happiness; it belonged by right to any face that sheltered in the bungalow.

She carried a child's parasol, which she was careful not to tear against the scrubby branches and bramble bushes as she sought for wild poppies along the edge of the fence. They were late poppies, a third generation, which had been unable to resist the call of the warm October sun.

Having gathered along one fence, she turned to cross to the opposite fence. Midway in the glade she came upon the tramp. Her startle was merely a startle. There was no fear in it. She stood and looked long and curiously at the forbidding spectacle, and was about to turn back when the sleeper moved restlessly and rolled his hand among the burrs. She noted the sun on his face, and the buzzing flies; her face grew solicitous, and for a moment she debated with herself. Then she tiptoed to his side, interposed the parasol between him and the sun, and brushed away the flies. After a time, for greater ease, she sat down beside him.

An hour passed, during which she occasionally shifted the parasol from one tired hand to the other. At first the sleeper had been restless, but, shielded from the flies and the sun, his breathing became gentler and his movements ceased. Several times, however, he really frightened her. The first was the worst, coming abruptly and without warning. "Christ! How deep! How deep!" the man murmured from some profound of dream. The parasol was agitated; but the little girl controlled herself and continued her self-appointed ministrations.

Another time it was a gritting of teeth, as of some intolerable agony. So terribly did the teeth crunch and grind together that it seemed they must crush into fragments. A little later he suddenly stiffened out. The hands clenched and the face set with the savage resolution of the dream. The eyelids trembled from the shock of the fantasy, seemed about to open, but did not. Instead, the lips muttered:

"No; no! And once more no. I won't peach." The lips paused, then went on. "You might as well tie me up, warden, and cut me to pieces. That's all you can get outa me—blood. That's all any of you-uns has ever got outa me in this hole."

After this outburst the man slept gently on, while the little girl still held the parasol aloft and looked down with a great wonder at the frowsy, unkempt creature, trying to reconcile it with the little part of life that she knew. To her ears came the cries of men, the stamp of hoofs on the bridge, and the creak and groan of wagons heavy laden. It was a breathless California Indian summer day. Light fleeces of cloud drifted in the azure sky, but to the west heavy cloud banks threatened with rain. A bee droned lazily by. From farther thickets came the calls of quail, and from the fields the songs of meadow larks. And oblivious to it all slept Ross Shanklin—Ross Shanklin, the tramp and outcast, ex-convict 4379, the bitter and unbreakable one who had defied all keepers and survived all brutalities.

Texas-born, of the old pioneer stock that was always tough and stubborn, he had been unfortunate. At seventeen years of age he had been apprehended for horse stealing. Also, he had been convicted of stealing seven horses which he had not stolen, and he had been sentenced to fourteen years' imprisonment. This was severe under any circumstances, but with him it had been especially severe, because there had been no prior convictions against him. The sentiment of the people who believed him guilty had been that two years was adequate punishment for the youth, but the county attorney, paid according to the convictions he secured, had made seven charges against him and earned seven fees. Which goes to show that the county attorney valued twelve years of Ross Shanklin's life at less than a few dollars.

Young Ross Shanklin had toiled terribly in jail; he had escaped, more than once; and he had been caught and sent back to toil in other and various jails. He had been triced up and lashed till he fainted had been revived and lashed again. He had been in the dungeon ninety days at a time. He had experienced the torment of the straightjacket. He knew what the humming bird was. He had been farmed out as a chattel by the state to the contractors. He had been trailed through swamps by bloodhounds. Twice he had been shot. For six years on end he had cut a cord and a half of wood each day in a convict lumber camp. Sick or well, he had cut that cord and a half or paid for it under a whip-lash knotted and pickled.

And Ross Shanklin had not sweetened under the treatment. He had sneered, and raved, and defied. He had seen convicts, after the guards had manhandled them, crippled in body for life, or left to maunder in mind to the end of their days. He had seen convicts, even his own cell mate, goaded to murder by their keepers, go to the gallows reviling God. He had been in a break in which eleven of his kind were shot down. He had been through a mutiny, where, in the prison yard, with gatling guns trained upon them, three hundred convicts had been disciplined with pick handles wielded by brawny guards.

He had known every infamy of human cruelty, and through it all he had never been broken. He had resented and fought to the last, until, embittered and bestial, the day came when he was discharged. Five dollars were given him in payment for the years of his labor and the flower of his manhood. And he had worked little in the years that followed. Work he hated and despised. He tramped, begged and stole, lied or threatened as the case might warrant, and drank to besottedness whenever he got the chance.

The little girl was looking at him when he awoke. Like a wild animal, all of him was awake the instant he opened his eyes. The first he saw was the parasol, strangely obtruded between him and the sky. He did not start nor move, though his whole body seemed slightly to tense. His eyes followed down the parasol handle to the tight-clutched little fingers, and along the arm to the child's face. Straight and unblinking he looked into her eyes, and she, returning the look, was chilled and frightened by his glittering eyes, cold and harsh, withal bloodshot, and with no hint in them of the warm humanness she had been accustomed to see and feel in human eyes. They were the true prison eyes—the eyes of a man who had learned to talk little, who had forgotten almost how to talk.

"Hello," he said finally, making no effort to change his position. "What game are you up to!"

His voice was gruff and husky, and at first it had been harsh; but it had softened queerly in a feeble attempt at forgotten kindliness.

"How do you do?" she said. "I'm not playing. The sun was on your face, and mamma says one oughtn't to sleep in the sun."

The sweet clearness of her child's voice was pleasant to him, and he wondered why he had never noticed it in children's voices before. He sat up slowly and stared at her. He felt that he ought to say something, but speech with him was a reluctant thing.

"I hope you slept well," she said gravely.

"I sure did," he answered, never taking his eyes from her, amazed at the fairness and delicacy of her. "How long was you holdin' that contraption up over me?"

"O-oh," she debated with herself, "a long, long time. I thought you would never wake up."

"And I thought you was a fairy when I first seen you."

He felt elated at his contribution to the conversation.

"No, not a fairy," she smiled.

He thrilled in a strange, numb way at the immaculate whiteness of her small even teeth.

"I was just the good Samaritan," she added.

"I reckon I never heard of that party."

He was cudgelling his brains to keep the conversation going. Never having been at close quarters with a child since he was man-grown, he found it difficult.

"What a funny man not to know about the good Samaritan. Don't you remember? A certain man went down to Jericho——"

"I reckon I've been there," he interrupted.

"I knew you were a traveler!" she cried, clapping her hands. "Maybe you saw the exact spot."

"What spot?"

"Why, where he fell among thieves and was left half dead. And then the good Samaritan went to him, and bound up his wounds, and poured in oil and wine—was that olive oil, do you think?"

He shook his head slowly.

"I reckon you got me there. Olive oil is something the dagoes cooks with. I never heard of it for busted heads."

She considered his statement for a moment.

"Well," she announced, "we use olive oil in our cooking, so we must be dagoes. I never knew what they were before. I thought it was slang."

"And the Samaritan dumped oil on his head," the tramp muttered reminiscently. "Seems to me I recollect a sky pilot sayin' something about that old gent. D'ye know, I've been looking for him off 'n on all my life, and never scared up hide nor hair of him. They ain't no more Samaritans."

"Wasn't I one!" she asked quickly.

He looked at her steadily, with a great curiosity and wonder. Her ear, by a movement exposed to the sun, was transparent. It seemed he could almost see through it. He was amazed at the delicacy of her coloring, at the blue of her eyes, at the dazzle of the sun-touched golden hair. And he was astounded by her fragility. It came to him that she was easily broken. His eye went quickly from his huge, gnarled paw to her tiny hand in which it seemed to him he could almost see the blood circulate. He knew the power in his muscles, and he knew the tricks and turns by which men use their bodies to ill-treat men. In fact, he knew little else, and his mind for the time ran in its customary channel. It was his way of measuring the beautiful strangeness of her. He calculated a grip, and not a strong one, that could grind her little fingers to pulp. He thought of fist blows he had given to men's heads, and received on his own head, and felt that the least of them could shatter hers like an egg-shell. He scanned her little shoulders and slim waist, and knew in all certitude that with his two hands he could rend her to pieces.

"Wasn't I one?" she insisted again.

He came back to himself with a shock—or away from himself, as the case happened. He was loath that the conversation should cease.

"What?" he answered. "Oh, yes; you bet you was a Samaritan, even if you didn't have no olive oil." He remembered what his mind had been dwelling on, and asked, "But ain't you afraid?"

"Of ... of me?" he added lamely.

She laughed merrily.

"Mamma says never to be afraid of anything. She says that if you're good, and you think good of other people, they'll be good, too."

"And you was thinkin' good of me when you kept the sun off," he marveled.

"But it's hard to think good of bees and nasty crawly things," she confessed.

"But there's men that is nasty and crawly things," he argued.

"Mamma says no. She says there's good in everyone.

"I bet you she locks the house up tight at night just the same," he proclaimed triumphantly.

"But she doesn't. Mamma isn't afraid of anything. That's why she lets me play out here alone when I want. Why, we had a robber once. Mamma got right up and found him. And what do you think! He was only a poor hungry man. And she got him plenty to eat from the pantry, and afterward she got him work to do."

Ross Shanklin was stunned. The vista shown him of human nature was unthinkable. It had been his lot to live in a world of suspicion and hatred, of evil-believing and evil-doing. It had been his experience, slouching along village streets at nightfall, to see little children, screaming with fear, run from him to their mothers. He had even seen grown women shrink aside from him as he passed along the sidewalk.

He was aroused by the girl clapping her hands as she cried out:

"I know what you are! You're an open air crank. That's why you were sleeping here in the grass."

He felt a grim desire to laugh, but repressed it.

"And that's what tramps are—open air cranks," she continued. "I often wondered. Mamma believes in the open air. I sleep on the porch at night. So does she. This is our land. You must have climbed the fence. Mamma lets me when I put on my climbers—they're bloomers, you know. But you ought to be told something. A person doesn't know when they snore because they're asleep. But you do worse than that. You grit your teeth. That's bad. Whenever you are going to sleep you must think to yourself, 'I won't grit my teeth, I won't grit my teeth,' over and over, just like that, and by and by you'll get out of the habit.

"All bad things are habits. And so are all good things. And it depends on us what kind our habits are going to be. I used to pucker my eyebrows—wrinkle them all up, but mamma said I must overcome that habit. She said that when my eyebrows were wrinkled it was an advertisement that my brain was wrinkled inside, and that it wasn't good to have wrinkles in the brain. And then she smoothed my eyebrows with her hand and said I must always think smooth—smooth inside, and smooth outside. And do you know, it was easy. I haven't wrinkled my brows for ever so long. I've heard about filling teeth by thinking. But I don't believe that. Neither does mamma."

She paused rather out of breath. Nor did he speak. Her flow of talk had been too much for him. Also, sleeping drunkenly, with open mouth, had made him very thirsty. But, rather than lose one precious moment, he endured the torment of his scorching throat and mouth. He licked his dry lips and struggled for speech.

"What is your name?" he managed at last.

"Joan."

She looked her own question at him, and it was not necessary to voice it.

"Mine is Ross Shanklin," he volunteered, for the first time in forgotten years giving his real name.

"I suppose you've traveled a lot."

"I sure have, but not as much as I might have wanted to."

"Papa always wanted to travel, but he was too busy at the office. He never could get much time. He went to Europe once with mamma. That was before I was born. It takes money to travel."

Ross Shanklin did not know whether to agree with this statement or not.

"But it doesn't cost tramps much for expenses," she took the thought away from him. "Is that why you tramp?"

He nodded and licked his lips.

"Mamma says it's too bad that men must tramp to look for work. But there's lots of work now in the country. All the farmers in the valley are trying to get men. Have you been working?"

He shook his head, angry with himself that he should feel shame at the confession when his savage reasoning told him he was right in despising work. But this was followed by another thought. This beautiful little creature was some man's child. She was one of the rewards of work.

"I wish I had a little girl like you," he blurted out, stirred by a sudden consciousness of passion for paternity. "I'd work my hands off. I ... I'd do anything."

She considered his case with fitting gravity.

"Then you aren't married?"

"Nobody would have me."

"Yes, they would, if ..."

She did not turn up her nose, but she favored his dirt and rags with a look of disapprobation he could not mistake.

"Go on," he half-shouted. "Shoot it into me. If I was washed—if I wore good clothes—if I was respectable—if I had a job and worked regular—if I wasn't what I am."

To each statement she nodded.

"Well, I ain't that kind," he rushed on. "I'm no good. I'm a tramp. I don't want to work, that's what. And I like dirt."

Her face was eloquent with reproach as she said, "Then you were only making believe when you wished you had a little girl like me?"

This left him speechless, for he knew, in all the depths of his new-found passion, that that was just what he did want.

With ready tact, noting his discomfort, she sought to change the subject.

"What do you think of God?" she asked. "I ain't never met him. What do you think about him?"

His reply was evidently angry, and she was frank in her disapproval.

"You are very strange," she said. "You get angry so easily. I never saw anybody before that got angry about God, or work, or being clean."

"He never done anything for me," he muttered resentfully. He cast back in quick review of the long years of toil in the convict camps and mines. "And work never done anything for me neither."

An embarrassing silence fell.

He looked at her, numb and hungry with the stir of the father-love, sorry for his ill temper, puzzling his brain for something to say. She was looking off and away at the clouds, and he devoured her with his eyes. He reached out stealthily and rested one grimy hand on the very edge of her little dress. It seemed to him that she was the most wonderful thing in the world. The quail still called from the coverts, and the harvest sounds seemed abruptly to become very loud. A great loneliness oppressed him.

"I'm ... I'm no good," he murmured huskily and repentantly.

But, beyond a glance from her blue eyes, she took no notice. The silence was more embarrassing than ever. He felt that he could give the world just to touch with his lips that hem of her dress where his hand rested. But he was afraid of frightening her. He fought to find something to say, licking his parched lips and vainly attempting to articulate something, anything.

"This ain't Sonoma Valley," he declared finally. "This is fairy land, and you're a fairy. Mebbe I'm asleep and dreaming. I don't know. You and me don't know how to talk together, because, you see, you're a fairy and don't know nothing but good things, and I'm a man from the bad, wicked world."

Having achieved this much, he was left gasping for ideas like a stranded fish.

"And you're going to tell me about the bad, wicked world," she cried, clapping her hands. "I'm just dying to know."

He looked at her, startled, remembering the wreckage of womanhood he had encountered on the sunken ways of life. She was no fairy. She was flesh and blood, and the possibilities of wreckage were in her as they had been in him even when he lay at his mother's breast. And there was in her eagerness to know.

"Nope," he said lightly, "this man from the bad, wicked world ain't going to tell you nothing of the kind. He's going to tell you of the good things in that world. He's going to tell you how he loved hosses when he was a shaver, and about the first hoss he straddled, and the first hoss he owned. Hosses ain't like men. They're better. They're clean—clean all the way through and back again. And, little fairy, I want to tell you one thing—there sure ain't nothing in the world like when you're settin' a tired hoss at the end of a long day, and when you just speak, and that tired animal lifts under you willing and hustles along. Hosses! They're my long suit. I sure dote on hosses. Yep. I used to be a cowboy once."

She clapped her hands in the way that tore so delightfully to his heart, and her eyes were dancing, as she exclaimed:

"A Texas cowboy! I always wanted to see one! I heard papa say once that cowboys are bow-legged. Are you?"

"I sure was a Texas cowboy," he answered. "But it was a long time ago. And I'm sure bow-legged. You see, you can't ride much when you're young and soft without getting the legs bent some. Why, I was only a three-year-old when I begun. He was a three-year-old, too, fresh-broken. I led him up alongside the fence, dumb to the top rail, and dropped on. He was a pinto, and a real devil at bucking, but I could do anything with him. I reckon he knowed I was only a little shaver. Some hosses knows lots more 'n' you think."

For half an hour Ross Shanklin rambled on with his horse reminiscences, never unconscious for a moment of the supreme joy that was his through the touch of his hand on the hem of her dress. The sun dropped slowly into the cloud bank, the quail called more insistently, and empty wagon after empty wagon rumbled back across the bridge. Then came a woman's voice.

"Joan! Joan!" it called. "Where are you, dear?"

The little girl answered, and Ross Shanklin saw a woman, clad in a soft, clinging gown, come through the gate from the bungalow. She was a slender, graceful woman, and to his charmed eyes she seemed rather to float along than walk like ordinary flesh and blood.

"What have you been doing all afternoon?" the woman asked, as she came up.

"Talking, mamma," the little girl replied. "I've had a very interesting time."

Ross Shanklin scrambled to his feet and stood watchfully and awkwardly. The little girl took the mother's hand, and she, in turn, looked at him frankly and pleasantly, with a recognition of his humanness that was a new thing to him. In his mind ran the thought: the woman who ain't afraid. Not a hint was there of the timidity he was accustomed to seeing in women's eyes. And he was quite aware, and never more so, of his bleary-eyed, forbidding appearance.

"How do you do?" she greeted him sweetly and naturally.

"How do you do, ma'am," he responded, unpleasantly conscious of the huskiness and rawness of his voice.

"And did you have an interesting time, too!" she smiled.

"Yes, ma'am. I sure did. I was just telling your little girl about hosses."

"He was a cowboy, once, mamma," she cried.

The mother smiled her acknowledgment to him, and looked fondly down at the little girl. The thought that came into Ross Shanklin's mind was the awfulness of the crime if any one should harm either of the wonderful pair. This was followed by the wish that some terrible danger should threaten, so that he could fight, as he well knew how, with all his strength and life, to defend them.

"You'll have to come along, dear," the mother said. "It's growing late." She looked at Ross Shanklin hesitantly. "Would you care to have something to eat?"

"No, ma'am, thanking you kindly just the same. I ... I ain't hungry."

"Then say good-bye, Joan," she counselled.

"Good-bye." The little girl held out her hand, and her eyes lighted roguishly. "Good-bye, Mr. Man from the bad, wicked world."

To him, the touch of her hand as he pressed it in his was the capstone of the whole adventure.

"Good-bye, little fairy," he mumbled. "I reckon I got to be pullin' along."

But he did not pull along. He stood staring after his vision until it vanished through the gate. The day seemed suddenly empty. He looked about him irresolutely, then climbed the fence, crossed the bridge, and slouched along the road. He was in a dream. He did not note his feet nor the way they led him. At times he stumbled in the dust-filled ruts.

A mile farther on, he aroused at the crossroads. Before him stood the saloon. He came to a stop and stared at it, licking his lips. He sank his hand into his pants pocket and fumbled a solitary dime. "God!" he muttered. "God!" Then, with dragging, reluctant feet, went on along the road.

He came to a big farm. He knew it must be big, because of the bigness of the house and the size and number of the barns and outbuildings. On the porch, in shirt sleeves, smoking a cigar, keen-eyed and middle-aged, was the farmer.

"What's the chance for a job!" Ross Shanklin asked.

The keen eyes scarcely glanced at him.

"A dollar a day and grub," was the answer.

Ross Shanklin swallowed and braced himself.

"I'll pick grapes all right, or anything. But what's the chance for a steady job? You've got a big ranch here. I know hosses. I was born on one. I can drive team, ride, plough, break, do anything that anybody ever done with hosses."

The other looked him over with an appraising, incredulous eye.

"You don't look it," was the judgment.

"I know I don't. Give me a chance. That's all. I'll prove it."

The farmer considered, casting an anxious glance at the cloud bank into which the sun had sunk.

"I'm short a teamster, and I'll give you the chance to make good. Go and get supper with the hands."

Ross Shanklin's voice was very husky, and he spoke with an effort.

"All right. I'll make good. Where can I get a drink of water and wash up?"

"JUST MEAT"

He strolled to the corner and glanced up and down the intersecting street, but saw nothing save the oases of light shed by the street lamps at the successive crossings. Then he strolled back the way he had come. He was a shadow of a man sliding noiselessly and without undue movement through the semi darkness. Also he was very alert, like a wild animal in the jungle, keenly perceptive and receptive. The movement of another in the darkness about him would need to have been more shadowy than he to have escaped him.

In addition to the running advertisement of the state of affairs carried to him by his senses, he had a subtler perception, a feel, of the atmosphere around him. He knew that the house in front of which he paused for a moment, contained children. Yet by no willed effort of perception did he have this knowledge. For that matter, he was not even aware that he knew, so occult was the impression. Yet, did a moment arise in which action, in relation to that house, were imperative, he would have acted on the assumption that it contained children. He was not aware of all that he knew about the neighborhood.

In the same way, he knew not how, he knew that no danger threatened in the footfalls that came up the cross street. Before he saw the walker, he knew him for a belated pedestrian hurrying home. The walker came into view at the crossing and disappeared on up the street. The man that watched, noted a light that flared up in the window of a house on the corner, and as it died down he knew it for an expiring match. This was conscious identification of familiar phenomena, and through his mind flitted the thought, "Wanted to know what time." In another house one room was lighted. The light burned dimly and steadily, and he had the feel that it was a sick room.

He was especially interested in a house across the street in the middle of the block. To this house he paid most attention. No matter what way he looked, nor what way he walked, his looks and his steps always returned to it. Except for an open window above the porch, there was nothing unusual about the house. Nothing came in nor out. Nothing happened. There were no lighted windows, nor had lights appeared and disappeared in any of the windows. Yet it was the central point of his consideration. He rallied to it each time after a divination of the state of the neighborhood.

Despite his feel of things, he was not confident. He was supremely conscious of the precariousness of his situation. Though unperturbed by the footfalls of the chance pedestrian, he was as keyed up and sensitive and ready to be startled as any timorous deer. He was aware of the possibility of other intelligences prowling about in the darkness—intelligences similar to his own in movement, perception, and divination.

Far down the street he caught a glimpse of something that moved. And he knew it was no late home-goer, but menace and danger. He whistled twice to the house across the street, then faded away shadow-like to the corner and around the corner. Here he paused and looked about him carefully. Reassured, he peered back around the corner and studied the object that moved and that was coming nearer. He had divined aright. It was a policeman.

The man went down the cross street to the next corner, from the shelter of which he watched the corner he had just left. He saw the policeman pass by, going straight on up the street. He paralleled the policeman's course, and from the next corner again watched him go by; then he returned the way he had come. He whistled once to the house across the street, and after a time whistled once again. There was reassurance in the whistle, just as there had been warning in the previous double whistle.

He saw a dark bulk outline itself on the roof of the porch and slowly descend a pillar. Then it came down the steps, passed through the small iron gate, and went down the sidewalk, taking on the form of a man. He that watched kept on his own side the street and moved on abreast to the corner, where he crossed over and joined the other. He was quite small alongside the man he accosted.

"How'd you make out, Matt?" he asked.

The other grunted indistinctly, and walked on in silence a few steps.

"I reckon I landed the goods," he said.

Jim chuckled in the darkness, and waited for further information. The blocks passed by; under their feet, and he grew impatient.

"Well, how about them goods?" he asked. "What kind of a haul did you make, anyway?"

"I was too busy to figger it out, but it's fat. I can tell you that much, Jim, it's fat. I don't dast to think how fat it is. Wait till we get to the room."

Jim looked at him keenly under the street lamp of the next crossing, and saw that his face was a trifle grim and that he carried his left arm peculiarly.

"What's the matter with your arm?" he demanded.

"The little cuss bit me. Hope I don't get hydrophoby. Folks gets hydrophoby from man-bite sometimes, don't they?"

"Gave you a fight, eh!" Jim asked encouragingly.

The other grunted.

"You're certainly hard to get information from," Jim burst out irritably. "Tell us about it. You ain't goin' to lose money just a-tellin' a guy."

"I guess I choked him some," came the answer. Then, by way of explanation, "He woke up on me."

"You did it neat. I never heard a sound."

"Jim," the other said with seriousness, "it's a hangin' matter. I fixed 'm. I had to. He woke up on me. You an' me's got to do some layin' low for a spell."

Jim gave a low whistle of comprehension.

"Did you hear me whistle!" he asked suddenly.

"Sure. I was all done. I was just comin' out."

"It was a bull. But he wasn't on a little bit. Went right by an' kept a-paddin' the hoof outa sight. Then I came back an' gave you the whistle. What made you take so long after that?"

"I was waitin' to make sure," Matt explained.

"I was mighty glad when I heard you whistle again. It's hard work waitin'. I just sat there an' thought an' thought ... oh, all kinds of things. It's remarkable what a fellow'll think about. And then there was a darn cat that kept movin' around the house an' botherin' me with its noises."

"An' it's fat!" Jim exclaimed irrelevantly and with joy.

"I'm sure tellin' you, Jim, it's fat. I'm plum' anxious for another look at 'em."

Unconsciously the two men quickened their pace. Yet they did not relax from their caution. Twice they changed their course in order to avoid policemen, and they made very sure that they were not observed when they dived into the dark hallway of a cheap rooming house down town.

Not until they had gained their own room on the top floor, did they scratch a match. While Jim lighted a lamp, Matt locked the door and threw the bolts into place. As he turned, he noticed that his partner was waiting expectantly. Matt smiled to himself at the other's eagerness.

"Them search-lights is all right," he said, drawing forth a small pocket electric lamp and examining it. "But we got to get a new battery. It's runnin' pretty weak. I thought once or twice it'd leave me in the dark. Funny arrangements in that house. I near got lost. His room was on the left, an' that fooled me some."

"I told you it was on the left," Jim interrupted.

"You told me it was on the right," Matt went on. "I guess I know what you told me, an' there's the map you drew."

Fumbling in his vest pocket, he drew out a folded slip of paper. As he unfolded it, Jim bent over and looked.

"I did make a mistake," he confessed.

"You sure did. It got me guessin' some for a while."

"But it don't matter now," Jim cried. "Let's see what you got."

"It does matter," Matt retorted. "It matters a lot ... to me. I've got to run all the risk. I put my head in the trap while you stay on the street. You got to get on to yourself an' be more careful. All right, I'll show you."

He dipped loosely into his trousers pocket and brought out a handful of small diamonds. He spilled them out in a blazing stream on the greasy table. Jim let out a great oath.

"That's nothing," Matt said with triumphant complacence. "I ain't begun yet."

From one pocket after another he continued bringing forth the spoil. There were many diamonds wrapped in chamois skin that were larger than those in the first handful. From one pocket he brought out a handful of very small cut gems.

"Sun dust," he remarked, as he spilled them on the table in a space by themselves.

Jim examined them.

"Just the same, they retail for a couple of dollars each," he said. "Is that all?"

"Ain't it enough?" the other demanded in an aggrieved tone.

"Sure it is," Jim answered with unqualified approval. "Better'n I expected. I wouldn't take a cent less than ten thousan' for the bunch."

"Ten thousan'," Matt sneered. "They're worth twic't that, an' I don't know anything about joolery, either. Look at that big boy!"

He picked it out from the sparkling heap and held it near to the lamp with the air of an expert, weighing and judging.

"Worth a thousan' all by its lonely," was Jim's quicker judgment.

"A thousan' your grandmother," was Matt's scornful rejoinder. "You couldn't buy it for three."

"Wake me up! I'm dreamin'!" The sparkle of the gems was in Jim's eyes, and he began sorting out the larger diamonds and examining them. "We're rich men, Matt—we'll be regular swells."

"It'll take years to get rid of 'em," was Matt's more practical thought.

"But think how we'll live! Nothin' to do but spend the money an' go on gettin' rid of 'em."

Matt's eyes were beginning to sparkle, though sombrely, as his phlegmatic nature woke up.

"I told you I didn't dast think how fat it was," he murmured in a low voice.

"What a killin'! What a killin'!" was the other's more ecstatic utterance.

"I almost forgot," Matt said, thrusting his hand into his inside coat pocket.

A string of large pearls emerged from wrappings of tissue paper and chamois skin. Jim scarcely glanced at them.

"They're worth money," he said, and returned to the diamonds.

A silence fell on the two men. Jim played with the gems, running them through his fingers, sorting them into piles, and spreading them out flat and wide. He was a slender, weazened man, nervous, irritable, high-strung, and anaemic—a typical child of the gutter, with unbeautiful twisted features, small eyes, with face and mouth perpetually and feverishly hungry, brutish in a catlike way, stamped to the core with degeneracy.

Matt did not finger the diamonds. He sat with chin on hands and elbows on table, blinking heavily at the blazing array. He was in every way a contrast to the other. No city had bred him. He was heavy muscled and hairy, gorilla-like in strength and aspect. For him there was no unseen world. His eyes were full and wide apart, and there seemed in them a certain bold brotherliness. They inspired confidence. But a closer inspection would have shown that his eyes were just a trifle too full, just a shade too wide apart. He exceeded, spilled over the limits of normality, and his features told lies about the man beneath.

"The bunch is worth fifty thousan'," Jim remarked suddenly.

"A hundred thousan'," Matt said.

The silence returned and endured a long time, to be broken again by Jim.

"What in blazes was he doin' with 'em all at the house?—that's what I want to know. I'd a-thought he'd kept 'em in the safe down at the store."

Matt had just been considering the vision of the throttled man as he had last looked upon him in the dim light of the electric lantern; but he did not start at the mention of him.

"There's no tellin'," he answered. "He might a-been getting ready to chuck his pardner. He might a-pulled out in the mornin' for parts unknown, if we hadn't happened along. I guess there's just as many thieves among honest men as there is among thieves. You read about such things in the papers, Jim. Pardners is always knifin' each other."

A queer, nervous look came in the other's eyes. Matt did not betray that he noted it, though he said:—

"What was you thinkin' about, Jim!"

Jim was a trifle awkward for the moment.

"Nothin'," he answered. "Only I was thinkin' just how funny it was—all them jools at his house. What made you ask?"

"Nothin'. I was just wonderin', that was all."

The silence settled down, broken by an occasional low and nervous giggle on the part of Jim. He was overcome by the spread of gems. It was not that he felt their beauty. He was unaware that they were beautiful in themselves. But in them his swift imagination visioned the joys of life they would buy, and all the desires and appetites of his diseased mind and sickly flesh were tickled by the promise they extended. He builded wondrous, orgy-haunted castles out of their brilliant fires, and was appalled at what he builded. Then it was that he giggled. It was all too impossible to be real. And yet there they blazed on the table before him, fanning the flame of the lust of him, and he giggled again.

"I guess we might as well count 'em," Matt said suddenly, tearing himself away from his own visions. "You watch me an' see that it's square, because you an' me has got to be on the square, Jim. Understand?"

Jim did not like this, and betrayed it in his eyes, while Matt did not like what he saw in his partner's eyes.

"Understand!" Matt repeated, almost menacingly.

"Ain't we always been square?" the other replied, on the defensive, what of the treachery already whispering in him.

"It don't cost nothin', bein' square in hard times," Matt retorted. "It's bein' square in prosperity that counts. When we ain't got nothin', we can't help bein' square. We're prosperous now, an' we've got to be business men—honest business men. Understand?"

"That's the talk for me," Jim approved, but deep down in the meagre soul of him,—and in spite of him,—wanton and lawless thoughts were stirring like chained beasts.

Matt stepped to the food shelf behind the two-burner kerosene cooking stove. He emptied the tea from a paper bag, and from a second bag emptied some red peppers. Returning to the table with the bags, he put into them the two sizes of small diamonds. Then he counted the large gems and wrapped them in their tissue paper and chamois skin.

"Hundred an' forty-seven good-sized ones," was his inventory; "twenty real big ones; two big boys and one whopper; an' a couple of fistfuls of teeny ones an' dust."

He looked at Jim.

"Correct," was the response.

He wrote the count out on a slip of memorandum paper, and made a copy of it, giving one slip to his partner and retaining the other.

"Just for reference," he said.

Again he had recourse to the food shelf, where he emptied the sugar from a large paper bag. Into this he thrust the diamonds, large and small, wrapped it up in a bandana handkerchief, and stowed it away under his pillow. Then he sat down on the edge of the bed and took off his shoes.

"An' you think they're worth a hundred thousan'?" Jim asked, pausing and looking up from the unlacing of his shoe.

"Sure," was the answer. "I seen a dancer down in Arizona once, with some big sparklers on her. They wasn't real. She said if they was she wouldn't be dancin'. Said they'd be worth all of fifty thousan', an' she didn't have a dozen of 'em all told."

"Who'd work for a livin'?" Jim triumphantly demanded. "Pick an' shovel work!" he sneered. "Work like a dog all my life, an' save all my wages, an' I wouldn't have half as much as we got to-night."

"Dish washin's about your measure, an' you couldn't get more'n twenty a month an' board. Your figgers is 'way off, but your point is well taken. Let them that likes it, work. I rode range for thirty a month when I was young an' foolish. Well, I'm older, an' I ain't ridin' range."

He got into bed on one side. Jim put out the light and followed him in on the other side.

"How's your arm feel?" Jim queried amiably.

Such concern was unusual, and Matt noted it, and replied:—

"I guess there's no danger of hydrophoby. What made you ask?"

Jim felt in himself a guilty stir, and under his breath he cursed the other's way of asking disagreeable questions; but aloud he answered: "Nothin', only you seemed scared of it at first. What are you goin' to do with your share, Matt?"

"Buy a cattle ranch in Arizona an' set down an' pay other men to ride range for me. There's some several I'd like to see askin' a job from me, blast them! An' now you shut your face, Jim. It'll be some time before I buy that ranch. Just now I'm goin' to sleep."

But Jim lay long awake, nervous and twitching, rolling about restlessly and rolling himself wide awake every time he dozed. The diamonds still blazed under his eyelids, and the fire of them hurt. Matt, in spite of his heavy nature, slept lightly, like a wild animal alert in its sleep; and Jim noticed, every time he moved, that his partner's body moved sufficiently to show that it had received the impression and that it was trembling on the verge of awakening. For that matter, Jim did not know whether or not, frequently, the other was awake. Once, quietly, betokening complete consciousness, Matt said to him: "Aw, go to sleep, Jim. Don't worry about them jools. They'll keep." And Jim had thought that at that particular moment Matt had been surely asleep.

In the late morning Matt was awake with Jim's first movement, and thereafter he awoke and dozed with him until midday, when they got up together and began dressing.

"I'm goin' out to get a paper an' some bread," Matt said. "You boil the coffee."

As Jim listened, unconsciously his gaze left Matt's face and roved to the pillow, beneath which was the bundle wrapped in the bandana handkerchief. On the instant Matt's face became like a wild beast's.

"Look here, Jim," he snarled. "You've got to play square. If you do me dirt, I'll fix you. Understand? I'd eat you, Jim. You know that. I'd bite right into your throat an' eat you like that much beefsteak."

His sunburned skin was black with the surge of blood in it, and his tobacco-stained teeth were exposed by the snarling lips. Jim shivered and involuntarily cowered. There was death in the man he looked at. Only the night before that black-faced man had killed another with his hands, and it had not hurt his sleep. And in his own heart Jim was aware of a sneaking guilt, of a train of thought that merited all that was threatened.

Matt passed out, leaving him still shivering. Then a hatred twisted his own face, and he softly hurled savage threats at the door. He remembered the jewels, and hastened to the bed, feeling under the pillow for the bandana bundle. He crushed it with his fingers to make certain that it still contained the diamonds. Assured that Matt had not carried them away, he looked toward the kerosene stove with a guilty start. Then he hurriedly lighted it, filled the coffee pot at the sink, and put it over the flame.

The coffee was boiling when Matt returned, and while the

latter cut the bread and put a slice of butter on the table, Jim poured out the coffee. It was not until he sat down and had taken a few sips of the coffee, that Matt pulled out the morning paper from his pocket.

"We was way off," he said. "I told you I didn't dast figger out how fat it was. Look at that."

He pointed to the head lines on the first page. "SWIFT NEMESIS ON BUJANNOFF'S TRACK," they read. "MURDERED IN HIS SLEEP AFTER ROBBING HIS PARTNER."

"There you have it!" Matt cried. "He robbed his partner—robbed him like a dirty thief."

"Half a million of jewels missin'," Jim read aloud. He put the paper down and stared at Matt.

"That's what I told you," the latter said. "What in thunder do we know about jools? Half a million!—an' the best I could figger it was a hundred thousan'. Go on an' read the rest of it."

They read on silently, their heads side by side, the untouched coffee growing cold; and ever and anon one or the other burst forth with some salient printed fact.

"I'd like to seen Metzner's face when he opened the safe at the store this mornin'," Jim gloated.

"He hit the high places right away for Bujannoff's house," Matt explained. "Go on an' read."

"Was to have sailed last night at ten on the Sajoda for the South Seas—steamship delayed by extra freight——"

"That's why we caught 'm in bed," Matt interrupted. "It was just luck—like pickin' a fifty-to-one winner."

"Sajoda sailed at six this mornin'——"

"He didn't catch her," Matt said. "I saw his alarm clock was set at five. That'd given 'm plenty of time ... only I come along an' put the kibosh on his time. Go on."

"Adolph Metzner in despair—the famous Haythorne pearl necklace—magnificently assorted pearls—valued by experts at from fifty to seventy thousan' dollars."

Jim broke off to say solemnly, "Those oyster-eggs worth all that money!"

He licked his lips and added, "They was beauties an' no mistake."

"Big Brazilian gem," he read on. "Eighty thousan' dollars—many valuable gems of the first water—several thousan' small diamonds well worth forty thousan'."

"What you don't know about jools is worth knowin'," Matt smiled good humoredly.

"Theory of the sleuths," Jim read. "Thieves must have known—cleverly kept watch on Bujannoff's actions—must have learned his plan and trailed him to his house with the fruits of his robbery—"

"Clever—" Matt broke out. "That's the way reputations is made ... in the noos-papers. How'd we know he was robbin' his pardner?"

"Anyway, we've got the goods," Jim grinned. "Let's look at 'em again."

He assured himself that the door was locked and bolted, while Matt brought out the bundle in the bandana and opened it on the table.

"Ain't they beauties, though!" Jim exclaimed at sight of the pearls; and for a time he had eyes only for them. "Accordin' to the experts, worth from fifty to seventy thousan' dollars."

"An' women like them things," Matt commented. "An' they'll do everything to get 'em—sell themselves, commit murder, anything."

"Just like you an' me."

"Not on your life," Matt retorted. "I'll commit murder for 'em, but not for their own sakes, but for the sake of what they'll get me. That's the difference. Women want the jools for themselves, an' I want the jools for the women an' such things they'll get me."

"Lucky that men an' women don't want the same things," Jim remarked.

"That's what makes commerce," Matt agreed; "people wantin' different things."

In the middle of the afternoon Jim went out to buy food. While he was gone, Matt cleared the table of the jewels, wrapping them up as before and putting them under the pillow. Then he lighted the kerosene stove and started to boil water for the coffee. A few minutes later, Jim returned.

"Most surprising," he remarked. "Streets, an' stores, an' people just like they always was. Nothin' changed. An' me walkin' along through it all a millionnaire. Nobody looked at me an' guessed it"

Matt grunted unsympathetically. He had little comprehension of the lighter whims and fancies of his partner's imagination.

"Did you get a porterhouse?" he demanded.

"Sure, an' an inch thick. It's a peach. Look at it."

He unwrapped the steak and held it up for the other's inspection. Then he made the coffee and set the table, while Matt fried the steak.

"Don't put on too much of them red peppers," Jim warned. "I ain't used to your Mexican cookin'. You always season too hot."

Matt grunted a laugh and went on with his cooking. Jim poured out the coffee, but first, into the nicked china cup, he emptied a powder he had carried in his vest pocket wrapped in a rice-paper. He had turned his back for the moment on his partner, but he did not dare to glance around at him. Matt placed a newspaper on the table, and on the newspaper set the hot frying pan. He cut the steak in half, and served Jim and himself.

"Eat her while she's hot," he counselled, and with knife and fork set the example.

"She's a dandy," was Jim's judgment, after his first mouthful. "But I tell you one thing straight. I'm never goin' to visit you on that Arizona ranch, so you needn't ask me."

"What's the matter now?" Matt asked.

"The Mexican cookin' on your ranch'd be too much for me. If I've got blue blazes a-comin' in the next life, I'm not goin' to torment my insides in this one!"

He smiled, expelled his breath forcibly to cool his burning mouth, drank some coffee, and went on eating the steak.

"What do you think about the next life anyway, Matt?" he asked a little later, while secretly he wondered why the other had not yet touched his coffee.

"Ain't no next life," Matt answered, pausing from the steak to take his first sip of coffee. "Nor heaven nor hell, nor nothin'. You get all that's comin' right here in this life."

"An' afterward?" Jim queried out of his morbid curiosity, for he knew that he looked upon a man that was soon to die. "An' afterward?" he repeated.

"Did you ever see a man two weeks dead?" the other asked.

Jim shook his head.

"Well, I have. He was like this beefsteak you an' me is eatin'. It was once steer cavortin' over the landscape. But now it's just meat. That's all, just meat. An' that's what you an' me an' all people come to—meat."

Matt gulped down the whole cup of coffee, and refilled the cup.

"Are you scared to die?" he asked.

Jim shook his head. "What's the use? I don't die anyway. I pass on an' live again—"

"To go stealin', an' lyin', an' snivellin' through another life, an' go on that way forever an' ever an' ever?" Matt sneered.

"Maybe I'll improve," Jim suggested hopefully. "Maybe stealin' won't be necessary in the life to come."

He ceased abruptly, and stared straight before him, a frightened expression on his face.

"What's the matter!" Matt demanded.

"Nothin'. I was just wonderin'"—Jim returned to himself with an effort—"about this dyin', that was all."

But he could not shake off the fright that had startled him. It was as if an unseen thing of gloom had passed him by, casting upon him the intangible shadow of its presence. He was aware of a feeling of foreboding. Something ominous was about to happen. Calamity hovered in the air. He gazed fixedly across the table at the other man. He could not understand. Was it that he had blundered and poisoned himself? No, Matt had the nicked cup, and he had certainly put the poison in the nicked cup.

It was all his own imagination, was his next thought. It had played him tricks before. Fool! Of course it was. Of course something was about to happen, but it was about to happen to Matt. Had not Matt drunk the whole cup of coffee?

Jim brightened up and finished his steak, sopping bread in the gravy when the meat was gone.

"When I was a kid—" he began, but broke off abruptly.

Again the unseen thing of gloom had fluttered, and his being was vibrant with premonition of impending misfortune. He felt a disruptive influence at work in the flesh of him, and in all his muscles there was a seeming that they were about to begin to twitch. He sat back suddenly, and as suddenly leaned forward with his elbows on the table. A tremor ran dimly through the muscles of his body. It was like the first rustling of leaves before the oncoming of wind. He clenched his teeth. It came again, a spasmodic tensing of his muscles. He knew panic at the revolt within his being. His muscles no longer recognized his mastery over them. Again they spasmodically tensed, despite the will of him, for he had willed that they should not tense. This was revolution within himself, this was anarchy; and the terror of impotence rushed up in him as his flesh gripped and seemed to seize him in a clutch, chills running up and down his back and sweat starting on his brow. He glanced about the room, and all the details of it smote him with a strange sense of familiarity. It was as though he had just returned from a long journey. He looked across the table at his partner. Matt was watching him and smiling. An expression of horror spread over Jim's face.

"Matt!" he screamed. "You ain't doped me?"

Matt smiled and continued to watch him. In the paroxysm that followed, Jim did not become unconscious. His muscles tensed and twitched and knotted, hurting him and crushing him in their savage grip. And in the midst of it all, it came to him that Matt was acting queerly. He was traveling the same road. The smile had gone from his face, and there was on it an intense expression, as if he were listening to some inner tale of himself and trying to divine the message. Matt got up and walked across the room and back again, then sat down.

"You did this, Jim," he said quietly.

"But I didn't think you'd try to fix me," Jim answered reproachfully.

"Oh, I fixed you all right," Matt said, with teeth close together and shivering body. "What did you give me?"

"Strychnine."

"Same as I gave you," Matt volunteered. "It's some mess, ain't it!"

"You're lyin', Matt," Jim pleaded. "You ain't doped me, have you?"

"I sure did, Jim; an' I didn't overdose you, neither. I cooked it in as neat as you please in your half the porterhouse.—Hold on! Where're you goin'?"

Jim had made a dash for the door, and was throwing back the bolts. Matt sprang in between and shoved him away.

"Drug store," Jim panted. "Drug store."

"No you don't. You'll stay right here. There ain't goin' to be any runnin' out an' makin' a poison play on the street—not with all them jools reposin' under the pillow. Savve? Even if you didn't die, you'd be in the hands of the police with a lot of explanations comin'. Emetics is the stuff for poison. I'm just as bad bit as you, an' I'm goin' to take a emetic. That's all they'd give you at a drug store, anyway."

He thrust Jim back into the middle of the room and shot the bolts into place. As he went across the floor to the food shelf, he passed one hand over his brow and flung off the beaded sweat. It spattered audibly on the floor. Jim watched agonizedly as Matt got the mustard can and a cup and ran for the sink. He stirred a cupful of mustard and water and drank it down. Jim had followed him and was reaching with trembling hands for the empty cup. Again Matt shoved him away. As he mixed a second cupful, he demanded:

"D'you think one cup'll do for me? You can wait till I'm done."

Jim started to totter toward the door, but Matt checked him.

"If you monkey with that door, I'll twist your neck. Savve? You can take yours when I'm done. An' if it saves you, I'll twist your neck, anyway. You ain't got no chance, nohow. I told you many times what you'd get if you did me dirt."

"But you did me dirt, too," Jim articulated with an effort.

Matt was drinking the second cupful, and did not answer. The sweat had got into Jim's eyes, and he could scarcely see his way to the table, where he got a cup for himself. But Matt was mixing a third cupful, and, as before, thrust him away.

"I told you to wait till I was done," Matt growled. "Get outa my way."

And Jim supported his twitching body by holding on to the sink, the while he yearned toward the yellowish concoction that stood for life. It was by sheer will that he stood and clung to the sink. His flesh strove to double him up and bring him to the floor. Matt drank the third cupful, and with difficulty managed to get to a chair and sit down. His first paroxysm was passing. The spasms that afflicted him were dying away. This good effect he ascribed to the mustard and water. He was safe, at any rate. He wiped the sweat from his face, and, in the interval of calm, found room for curiosity. He looked at his partner.

A spasm had shaken the mustard can out of Jim's hands, and the contents were spilled upon the floor. He stooped to scoop some of the mustard into the cup, and the succeeding spasm doubled him up on the floor. Matt smiled.

"Stay with it," he encouraged. "It's the stuff all right. It's fixed me up."

Jim heard him and turned toward him with a stricken face, twisted with suffering and pleading. Spasm now followed spasm till he was in convulsions, rolling on the floor and yellowing his face and hair in the mustard.

Matt laughed hoarsely at the sight, but the laugh broke midway. A tremor had run through his body. A new paroxysm was beginning. He arose and staggered across to the sink, where, with probing forefinger, he vainly strove to assist the action of the emetic. In the end, he clung to the sink as Jim had clung, filled with the horror of going down to the floor.

The other's paroxysm had passed, and he sat up, weak and fainting, too weak to rise, his forehead dripping, his lips flecked with a foam made yellow by the mustard in which he had rolled. He rubbed his eyes with his knuckles, and groans that were like whines came from his throat.

"What are you snifflin' about!" Matt demanded out of his agony. "All you got to do is die. An' when you die you're dead."

"I ... ain't ... snifflin' ... it's ... the ... mustard ... stingin' ... my ... eyes," Jim panted with desperate slowness.

It was his last successful attempt at speech. Thereafter he babbled incoherently, pawing the air with shaking arms till a fresh convulsion stretched him on the floor.

Matt struggled back to the chair, and, doubled up on it, with his arms clasped about his knees, he fought with his disintegrating flesh. He came out of the convulsion cool and weak. He looked to see how it went with the other, and saw him lying motionless.

He tried to soliloquize, to be facetious, to have his last grim laugh at life, but his lips made only incoherent sounds. The thought came to him that the emetic had failed, and that nothing remained but the drug store. He looked toward the door and drew himself to his feet. There he saved himself from falling by clutching the chair. Another paroxysm had begun. And in the midst of the paroxysm, with his body and all the parts of it flying apart and writhing and twisting back again into knots, he clung to the chair and shoved it before him across the floor. The last shreds of his will were leaving him when he gained the door. He turned the key and shot back one bolt. He fumbled for the second bolt, but failed. Then he leaned his weight against the door and slid down gently to the floor.

A NOSE FOR THE KING

In the morning calm of Korea, when its peace and tranquility truly merited its ancient name, "Cho-sen," there lived a politician by name Yi Chin Ho. He was a man of parts, and—who shall say?—perhaps in no wise worse than politicians the world over. But, unlike his brethren in other lands, Yi Chin Ho was in jail. Not that he had inadvertently diverted to himself public moneys, but that he had inadvertently diverted too much. Excess is to be deplored in all things, even in grafting, and Yi Chin Ho's excess had brought him to most deplorable straits.

Ten thousand strings of cash he owed the government, and he lay in prison under sentence of death. There was one advantage to the situation—he had plenty of time in which to think. And he thought well. Then called he the jailer to him.

"Most worthy man, you see before you one most wretched," he began. "Yet all will be well with me if you will but let me go free for one short hour this night. And all will be well with you, for I shall see to your advancement through the years, and you shall come at length to the directorship of all the prisons of Cho-sen."

"How now?" demanded the jailer. "What foolishness is this? One short hour, and you but waiting for your head to be chopped off! And I, with an aged and much-to-be-respected mother, not to say anything of a wife and several children of tender years! Out upon you for the scoundrel that you are!"

"From the Sacred City to the ends of all the Eight Coasts there is no place for me to hide," Yi Chin Ho made reply. "I am a man of wisdom, but of what worth my wisdom here in prison? Were I free, well I know I could seek out and obtain the money wherewith to repay the government. I know of a nose that will save me from all my difficulties."

"A nose!" cried the jailer.

"A nose," said Yi Chin Ho. "A remarkable nose, if I may say so, a most remarkable nose."

The jailer threw up his hands despairingly. "Ah, what a wag you are, what a wag," he laughed. "To think that that very admirable wit of yours must go the way of the chopping-block!"

And so saying, he turned and went away. But in the end, being a man soft of head and heart, when the night was well along he permitted Yi Chin Ho to go.

Straight he went to the Governor, catching him alone and arousing him from his sleep.

"Yi Chin Ho, or I'm no Governor!" cried the Governor. "What do you here who should be in prison waiting on the chopping-block!"

"I pray your excellency to listen to me," said Yi Chin Ho, squatting on his hams by the bedside and lighting his pipe from the fire-box. "A dead man is without value. It is true, I am as a dead man, without value to the government, to your excellency, or to myself. But if, so to say, your excellency were to give me my freedom—"

"Impossible!" cried the Governor. "Besides, you are condemned to death."

"Your excellency well knows that if I can repay the ten thousand strings of cash, the government will pardon me," Yi Chin Ho went on. "So, as I say, if your excellency were to give me my freedom for a few days, being a man of understanding, I should then repay the government and be in position to be of service to your excellency. I should be in position to be of very great service to your excellency."

"Have you a plan whereby you hope to obtain this money?" asked the Governor.

"I have," said Yi Chin Ho.

"Then come with it to me to-morrow night; I would now sleep," said the Governor, taking up his snore where it had been interrupted.

On the following night, having again obtained leave of absence from the jailer, Yi Chin Ho presented himself at the Governor's bedside.

"Is it you, Yi Chin Ho?" asked the Governor. "And have you the plan?"

"It is I, your excellency," answered Yi Chin Ho, "and the plan is here."

"Speak," commanded the Governor.

"The plan is here," repeated Yi Chin Ho, "here in my hand."

The Governor sat up and opened his eyes, Yi Chin Ho proffered in his hand a sheet of paper. The Governor held it to the light.

"Nothing but a nose," said he.

"A bit pinched, so, and so, your excellency," said Yi Chin Ho.

"Yes, a bit pinched here and there, as you say," said the Governor.

"Withal it is an exceeding corpulent nose, thus, and so, all in one place, at the end," proceeded Yi Chin Ho. "Your excellency would seek far and wide and many a day for that nose and find it not."

"An unusual nose," admitted the Governor.

"There is a wart upon it," said Yi Chin Ho.

"A most unusual nose," said the Governor. "Never have I seen the like. But what do you with this nose, Yi Chin Ho!"

"I seek it whereby to repay the money to the government," said Yi Chin Ho. "I seek it to be of service to your excellency, and I seek it to save my own worthless head. Further, I seek your excellency's seal upon this picture of the nose."

And the Governor laughed and affixed the seal of state, and Yi Chin Ho departed. For a month and a day he traveled the King's Road which leads to the shore of the Eastern Sea; and there, one night, at the gate of the largest mansion of a wealthy city he knocked loudly for admittance.

"None other than the master of the house will I see," said he fiercely to the frightened servants. "I travel upon the King's business."

Straightway was he led to an inner room, where the master of the house was roused from his sleep and brought blinking before him.

"You are Pak Chung Chang, head man of this city," said Yi Chin Ho in tones that were all-accusing. "I am upon the King's business."

Pak Chung Chang trembled. Well he knew the King's business was ever a terrible business. His knees smote together, and he near fell to the floor.

"The hour is late," he quavered. "Were it not well to——"

"The King's business never waits!" thundered Yi Chin Ho. "Come apart with me, and swiftly. I have an affair of moment to discuss with you.

"It is the King's affair," he added with even greater fierceness; so that Pak Chung Chang's silver pipe dropped from his nerveless fingers and clattered on the floor.

"Know then," said Yi Chin Ho, when they had gone apart, "that the King is troubled with an affliction, a very terrible affliction. In that he failed to cure, the Court physician has had nothing else than his head chopped off. From all the Eight Provinces have the physicians come to wait upon the King. Wise consultation have they held, and they have decided that for a remedy for the King's affliction nothing else is required than a nose, a certain kind of nose, a very peculiar certain kind of nose.

"Then by none other was I summoned than his excellency the prime minister himself. He put a paper into my hand. Upon this paper was the very peculiar kind of nose drawn by the physicians of the Eight Provinces, with the seal of state upon it.

"'Go,' said his excellency the prime minister. 'Seek out this nose, for the King's affliction is sore. And wheresoever you find this nose upon the face of a man, strike it off forthright and bring it in all haste to the Court, for the King must be cured. Go, and come not back until your search is rewarded.'

"And so I departed upon my quest," said Yi Chin Ho. "I have sought out the remotest corners of the kingdom; I have traveled the Eight Highways, searched the Eight Provinces, and sailed the seas of the Eight Coasts. And here I am."

With a great flourish he drew a paper from his girdle, unrolled it with many snappings and cracklings, and thrust it before the face of Pak Chung Chang. Upon the paper was the picture of the nose.

Pak Chung Chang stared upon it with bulging eyes.

"Never have I beheld such a nose," he began.

"There is a wart upon it," said Yi Chin Ho.

"Never have I beheld——" Pak Chung Chang began again.

"Bring your father before me," Yi Chin Ho interrupted sternly.

"My ancient and very-much-to-be-respected ancestor sleeps," said Pak Chung Chang.

"Why dissemble?" demanded Yi Chin Ho. "You know it is your father's nose. Bring him before me that I may strike it off and be gone. Hurry, lest I make bad report of you."

"Mercy!" cried Pak Chung Chang, falling on his knees. "It is impossible! It is impossible! You cannot strike off my father's nose. He cannot go down without his nose to the grave. He will become a laughter and a byword, and all my days and nights will be filled with woe. O reflect! Report that you have seen no such nose in your travels. You, too, have a father."

Pak Chung Chang clasped Yi Chin Ho's knees and fell to weeping on his sandals.

"My heart softens strangely at your tears," said Yi Chin Ho. "I, too, know filial piety and regard. But—" He hesitated, then added, as though thinking aloud, "It is as much as my head is worth."

"How much is your head worth?" asked Pak Chung Chang in a thin, small voice.

"A not remarkable head," said Yi Chin Ho. "An absurdly unremarkable head! but, such is my great foolishness, I value it at nothing less than one hundred thousand strings of cash."

"So be it," said Pak Chung Chang, rising to his feet.

"I shall need horses to carry the treasure," said Yi Chin Ho, "and men to guard it well as I journey through the mountains. There are robbers abroad in the land."

"There are robbers abroad in the land," said Pak Chung Chang, sadly. "But it shall be as you wish, so long as my ancient and very-much-to-be-respected ancestor's nose abide in its appointed place."

"Say nothing to any man of this occurrence," said Yi Chin Ho, "else will other and more loyal servants than I be sent to strike off your father's nose."

And so Yi Chin Ho departed on his way through the mountains, blithe of heart and gay of song as he listened to the jingling bells of his treasure-laden ponies.

There is little more to tell. Yi Chin Ho prospered through the years. By his efforts the jailer attained at length to the directorship of all the prisons of Cho-sen; the Governor ultimately betook himself to the Sacred City to be prime minister to the King, while Yi Chin Ho became the King's boon companion and sat at table with him to the end of a round, fat life. But Pak Chung Chang fell into a melancholy, and ever after he shook his head sadly, with tears in his eyes, whenever he regarded the expensive nose of his ancient and very-much-to-be-respected ancestor.

www.ingramcontent.com/pod-product-compliance
Lightning Source LLC
Chambersburg PA
CBHW011514170626
46810CB00009B/3356
* 9 7 8 1 6 4 7 9 9 4 8 8 4 *